THE BAGUA AND OTHER STORIES

The Bagua and Other Stories

LEENNA NAIDOO

Tall Fin Publishing

978-0-6397-1605-3

First Printing, 2022

First Digital Edition 2017

FIRST PUBLICATION INFORMATION

On Conveying...Solar System © Leena Naidoo 2015. First publication: *Mad Scientist Journal* Winter 2016.

Out Of Brambles © Leena Naidoo. First Publication 2015: *Cosmic Roots And Eldritch Shores* March 2016.

Unalienable Right © Leena Naidoo 2015. First Publication: *SciPhi Journal* May 2016.

Confessions of a Shape-shifter: All Aussie Family © Leena Naidoo 2016. First publication: Sweek.com 2017

Confessions of a Shape-shifter: Hawk-Eyed © Leena Naidoo 2016. First publication: Sweek.com 2017

Souls Provider © Leena Naidoo 2016. First publication: Sweek.com 2017

Substitute Ice-cream © Leena Naidoo 2016. First publication: Sweek.com 2017

The BaGua © Leena Naidoo 2010. First publication: Sweek.com 2017

Badly Drawn Lines © Leena Naidoo 2015. First publication: LARCscifi.com 2017

Love Like Water © Leena Naidoo 2015. First publication: www.leennanaidoo.wordpress.com 2015

Split Infinite © Leena Naidoo 2015. First publication: Quantum Shorts.com 2015

Switch Twitch © Leena Naidoo 2015. First publication: Quantum Shorts.com 2015

Amusement © Leena Naidoo 2011. First publication: *SeeThroughIt Magazine Mini* 2015

Martinus Meerkat Man © Leena Naidoo 2010. First publication: *SeeThroughIt Magazine* 2015

CONTENTS PAGE

Short Stories

Amusement

He would have been just as beautiful standing in a midden or a coal-pit. Beauty, in all its forms, was in his nature. As was deception. But like its very nature—like his very nature—you didn't notice it until it was too late.

Even the Faery Queen can meet her match.

The Bagua

She's been searching for dragons and he's been searching for a magical place. When these friends find the right BaGua, only the wondrous can happen.

A finalist in the #Sweeklove competition.

Bonus Story

The Walpole Were

Sighting: Possible Canid. Likely a werewolf

Location: Walpole, Western Australia

Status: Developing—tracking and research

When Stacy hires a cabin at in the quiet Walpole forest, the last creature she expects to meet is a wolf. Now he's got evil designs on her, but he hasn't counted on the locals' personal interest in matters.

ACKNOWLEDGEMENTS

My great thanks to the editors of the magazines that published my work, for taking a chance on a newbie writer who didn't always know what she was doing; in particular to Dawn Vogel, Jeremy Zimmerman, Fran Eisenmann, and Jason Rennie. And not forgetting S.Shane Thomas for putting up my one-and-only Anunnaki character. All continuing errors are my own or for effect.

My immense thanks to beta-reader Elizabeth Aiko who gave me faith in stories I'd been led to believe were no good or lacked humour, the Critters over at Critters.org, and the following who always provide me with the support, belief and encouragement I need to keep writing and trying my best: Mum, Miranda, Rani and Suren, Lorraine, Cretia (for reading), Lisa (for listening), Kuban and Ramola, Sam T, plus my sister who'd wanted her print copies and my awesome patrons past and present. And to all of you who read my books and stories!

Lots of love
Leenna
August 2022

SCIENCE FICTION SHORT STORY: LOCATION, WESTERN AUSTRALIA

UNALIENABLE RIGHT

It's a dirty job...

Looking down its long snooty nose with pursed lips, it said, "Come with me."You don't argue with a talking kangaroo when you're a lone woman in the desert; but I wanted to.

Nostrils flaring in distaste, it bounced off a short way. Leaving my beer, I hurried over, swerving around scrubs the marsupial hopped over. I was smarter than it, wasn't I?

"Now what?"

Snooty gripped my wrists with his paws, and it was all Beam me up, Snooty.

It wasn't what I'd expected, but I'd expected more than some old Trekkie rip-off.

The room—board or council, whatever—was another matter. Distinguished kangaroos murmured in the transparent chamber. The Earth hung like a giant mobile in the testosterone-filled air, or the roo equivalent.

The tallest kangaroo turned to me; his light brown eyes unwelcoming to a bedraggled geologist. "Ms Sharman, we care a lot," said the leader, his voice authoritative.

"That's nice."

"We care a lot about that environment. We

care even more for our...creations. We won't tolerate their destruction."

Confounded, I stared up at the pointing red kangaroo. "What?"

"Those new minerals you have discovered," began Snooty, "they belong to *us*."

"But..." My brain kicked in. This wasn't a fieldie matter. "You'll have to talk with our legal department and cultural officer," I explained. "They're the ones who handle compensation claims." All I wanted was my cold beer—a geologist's unalienable right to brewed sustenance.

The leader spoke again. "I don't think you understand, Ms Sharman. *We own* the intellectual patent of that mineral in this galaxy. It helps with the development of our creations."

I tried my blank look again, thankful I wasn't on the WALKMM legal team.

The leader continued. "You see, Ms Sharman, where your species plants flags on newly discovered lands, we plant life, replicas of ourselves, and minerals; gently edging worlds into acceptable realms of intelligence and productivity."

The mood in the room had gone cold. Like Snooty's long stare. "Look, I'm just the local geo—"

"And we care *a lot* about our creations. So much so..." The leader leaned closer, staring at me down that barrel of a nose. "...that we are prepared to destroy *all* our assets here to prevent little upstarts stealing them."

There was a murmur of approval around the room.

"And your...'world', will be quite destroyed in the process."

His fiery brown eyes bore into mine.

"Ah. Hmm...Well, I understand." I did too. You don't argue with kangaroos in the outback, never mind on their spaceship or whatever.

I cleared my throat. "I'm sure we can come to a...a solution."

"We are glad to see you care *enough*."

I was dismissed. Snooty beamed me down to my beer.

I swigged at my unalienable right, watching my field-report explode in my campfire. You don't argue over intergalactic intellectual property when the fall-out would leave your work extinct.

It's a dirty job, but someone's got to do it. Whatever.

###

This story first appeared in SciPhi Journal in 2016 (editor Jason Rennie) with an illustration by Cat Leonard.

FANTASY: LOCATION, SOUTH AFRICAN COAST

A Tanker's Soul

Whales are ever kind-hearted and big on interventions.
And an intervention was exactly what the old reddish-brown tanker needed.

The young whale lay hidden under the olivine-coloured water. An eye rolled at the tanker sliding by. While the whale knew the Indian Ocean was big enough for all, the tanker did not and stuck to an erratic course plotted by GPS and echo-sounders. The young whale also knew that was no way to live. What was the fun in never exploring, in letting life slide by, in working alone the life-long day...?Whales are ever kind-hearted and big on interventions. And an intervention was exactly what the old reddish-brown tanker needed.

The young whale decided on the only proper course of action: to sing a song of freedom and awaken the soul of the tanker. It opened its big heart and sang.

***

The stranded tanker remained beached for months. Each day without fail the young whale came to sing a song of freedom, a song of life, and a song of remembrance carried to the body of the tanker by the caressing waves. Until, one day, its pod and its instincts told it of other work to be done.

Each day the tanker fell further apart, even as its soul was birthed and nourished. Each day, small sea-life found more and more homes in it. Gradually the tanker became more of the sea and the earth, its soul growing in unexpected and nurturing ways.

The storm of the century proved the tanker's next saviour. It washed the hull further out to sea, settling the tanker into a cosy channel not far from the breakers.

The tanker creaked its tired old hull and settled comfortably down with contentment. The kind whale had sung its soul into being, and the storm had given it the next great gift—the freedom to express itself as a nurturing soul and be one with life.

A never-before published micro-fiction written for the prompt 'submerged' and inspired by the Umhlanga and North coast in Durban, South Africa.

FANTASY: LOCATION, CHINA

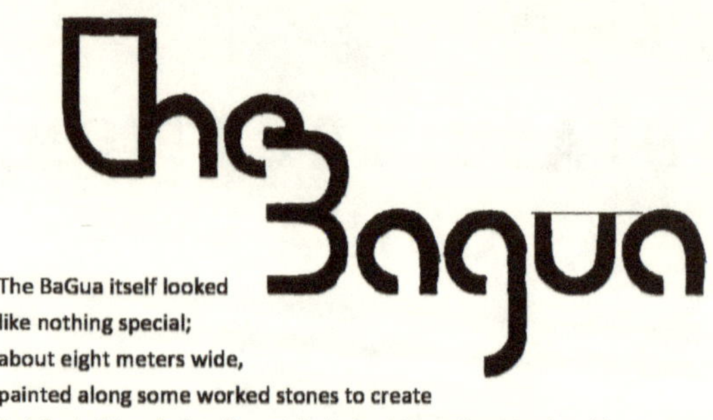

The BaGua itself looked
like nothing special;
about eight meters wide,
painted along some worked stones to create
its labyrinthine design. Except for being bigger than usual and less ornate
and intricate than most, it was much like all the other BaGuas we'd visited.

"We have to climb up that?" I panted. That was what looked like an impossible stairway rising at about seventy-five degrees straight up into the cerulean sky. A stairway to heaven—or to nowhere.

He nodded.

"Why don't I just wait here," I said, collapsing onto the warm stone stair and starting to dig out my water-bottle from my backpack, "...while you go on?"

"Chicken," he teased, coming back down to sit next to me.

We sat in easy silence in the hot sun, a cool breeze making it surprisingly pleasant. Below us the valley dozed, the river only just visible as a glittering trail in the green corn and sunflower fields.

We'd already climbed a fair way; first from the road to this remote imposing temple, then from the courtyard up another steep staircase to the main shrine and sacred spring, all of which now lay quietly below us. It was the spring water we drank, slightly salty but still refreshing.

"It's good for you!" the keeper of the spring had told us. "It will bring you good fortune."

Ken had translated for me. Despite being in China for over a year, I still hadn't mastered basic conversation. Numbers and my food, yes; conversation, no. Or symbols and writing.

Not for the first time, I wondered why I was continuing to stay in China. I'd come looking for something, believing a year would be enough. I hadn't yet found it, probably never would... Still, here I was sitting on another remote temple staircase. I'd stopped hoping already; stopped believing even. To continue searching had become my habit. At least it got me out into the countryside.

I was becoming a connoisseur of Chinese temples with their varied and harmonious shrines— many gods of many faiths happy enough to share the same mountain and followers. That's what really made them gods, not people.

"C'mon." Ken tapped me on the shoulder, stood up and stretched. "I've got a good feeling about this place. At the very least, you'll be sure to find some narrow stone tunnel you can struggle through."

He'd been quick to learn my weaknesses. Less than three weeks and he already knew I couldn't resist worn ancient stone steps nor buildings that were older than those back home in South Africa.

Shaking my head in amusement, I hefted my backpack and followed him up. It's best not to look too far up ahead or down. This wasn't the highest mountain in China but vertigo didn't know that.

I pondered about Ken again. He'd recently arrived in Yulin to work at the oil and gas sites as an environmentalist. We'd met in Central Square, so named because it was in the old city centre. I'd been reading whilst soaking up the sun. He'd been walking by. He probably would have continued on if I hadn't absentmindedly said *voetsek* to an annoying fly.

He'd laughed, backtracking. "You're South African!" His grin showed his delight.

"Ya. Are you?"

He wasn't; his cousin was. Ken was a New Zealander—the first intriguing fact I learned about him, with a new one following almost everyday.

"May I buy you a tea in exchange for some...*skinner?*"

"*Skinder,*" I corrected him, as I considered his offer of gossip.

He was handsome, not cute. I could see he was genuine, not just putting on an act. I liked the way the light caught his clear eyes and made them dance.

"Sure," I found myself saying out loud.

He smiled. "Great! Now, where would be the best place to find a cup of tea?"

We hit it off almost immediately. Ken didn't fit into the herd either like most of the other foreigners I'd met. They tended to bleat the same things, run around mindlessly annoying the locals with their drunken unfunny remarks and behaviour, looking with skewered judgemental eyes at everything they saw.

Ken was anything but a sheep. He had energy and magnetism which shone through even when he was down. It was so very strong that often I'd find myself just basking in it. He was curious, fair, and a fast learner. We laughed at the same absurdities, enjoyed the same music, believed similar things and debated everything else. He was inspiring, comforting, yet challenging to be around.

"Why are you here?" He was picking at fries as we sat in KFC.

"I'm teaching," I replied, putting my cup of tea down.

"No, I mean, why are you really here—in Yulin?"

I hadn't yet learned just how uncanny he could be. I shifted uncomfortably, having grown accustomed to being on my guard around other foreigners in China, and mindful of Yulin running on tiny village rules for foreigners. So I said, "Oh, you know...new culture and all that."

He wasn't buying it. Ken fixed me with those thoughtful eyes. "Fair's fair, I suppose. I should tell you my reason for being here."

He'd surprised me again. "You know you don't have to. That's your own business."

"I'm searching for a special BaGua—the Yin-Yang symbol. It's said to be around here at one of the temples."

"What's so special about it?"

"They say if you walk it, it will transform you and heal you."

"You need to be healed?" I was intrigued.

He nodded slowly, then leaned in closer. "I have this block—a psychic block, or injury if you prefer. And that is the remedy."

"Walking the BaGua?"

"Yeah." His eyes didn't falter.

Tilting my head, I considered him. I'd heard stranger things having hung out with some alternative life-stylers back home. "All right," I finally said.

He smiled again. "Good. Then you don't think I'm insane."

"No, just a little strange."

He grinned back.

It seemed only fair that I told him my real reason for being in China. "I'm searching for a dragon—a real live one."

"Like Bruce Lee?"

"No, a real *Lung* that can change the weather and stuff."

"Why?"

I shrugged, "Just." I honestly didn't know why myself.

"So...We can help each other on our quests," he smiled. "It'll be fun!"

And it was. I enjoyed taking him to the temples I knew in the city, from the famous Hong Xe Xia in the north to the one with the beautiful gardens in the south. Together we examined the architecture and paintings, inspected every BaGua we encountered, and asked countless questions of the obliging priests and keepers.

Afterwards was our time to discuss the temple visit over tea and move on to other topics. No wonder I fell in love with him though he never seemed anything more than affectionate to me. If he loved me he'd let me know in time, I reasoned. Meanwhile, I'd keep looking for dragons.

***

The stairway to the heavens led to a landing, which curved then rose further up to the levelled summit. The shrine was locked. I wished Wang Li, my friend who had told us of this little known temple and who had directed us here, could have accompanied us.

Ken walked around, taking it all in. Behind the shrine ran a narrow path, through brush and wild-flowers, leading to a bell—a massively gorgeous bronze one with two reptilian guards crowning it.

"Shall we?" asked Ken.

"Why not?" I was thrilled at the notion.

We rung the bell by pulling back on the heavy wooden pole and letting it swing. The bell pealed a deep sonorous note into the lonely hills. A minute or so later, all settled into peacefulness again with just the wind and us.

Ken snap out of a reverie. "Now, where's this BaGua?"

"What's that?" I pointed to the left where a balustrade peeped out.

Ken's grin was huge. "That's got to be it!" He hurried off. I followed at a more leisurely pace.

***

The balustrade enclosed a slightly sunken amphitheatre beyond which was a steep drop to the fields. The BaGua lay in the middle of the open clear space. In front of it stood a large stone incense burner filled with ash and a few dispirited red papers. Ken placed his small offering of incense in the burner.

The BaGua itself looked like nothing special; about eight meters wide, painted along some worked stones to create its labyrinthine design. Except for being bigger than usual and less ornate and intricate than most, it was much like all the other BaGuas we'd visited. Ken had crouched down, inspecting the BaGua.

I set my bag down near the outermost line next to his. "You think this is it?"

He didn't reply immediately. "I think it might be. Only one way to find out."

"Well, go on then." I smiled encouragement.

He stood up slowly like he was almost afraid to take the first step. Then he looked at me with a lopsided smile and took a deliberate step in.

I shivered, watching him. The breeze had picked up. It would be a strong wind soon. Ken, in growing meditation and highlighted by the bright sunlight, began to walk the BaGua.

I sat down on the warm stone floor next to my bag and waited quietly admiring his form, the clouds, and thinking arbitrary inconsequential thoughts. Time lost relevance with only the temperature of the wind to mark it. I pulled on a sweater, beginning to feel the chill in the air.

He was almost to the centre when the wind changed tone, taking on a sonorous quality, almost as if we were standing inside the bell. I stood up alarmed and looked around.

The day had changed.

Clouds scudded across the darkening sky though the wind-speed felt constant. The air took on a heavy quality; pressure building. The ground seemed to tremble. An earthquake?

"Ken!"

He couldn't hear me. Space appeared to have stretched. He seemed a long way away, although he must have only been four metres or so from me.

"Ken!" I screamed again. It was no use. My voice was too weak against the elements building up.

Should I also step into the BaGua to warn him? Static electricity had begun building up as if a giant Van De Graaff's generator had been turned on. My hair lifted into shocked tendrils that would have made Einstein envious.

"Ken!" I screamed once more, knowing it would be futile. I remained in an agony of indecision. I really didn't want to go into the BaGua. I was too scared. Why hadn't Ken noticed?

He stepped into the centre. I expected lightning to flash or something equally dramatic. Instead, Ken just collapsed.

***

I didn't realize I was running through the BaGua until the resistance began pushing me back so I was hardly moving. I'd only managed to cut across about a quarter of the way to its centre.

Ken was still lying prone. I couldn't reach him this way, fighting to take each small step. Turning to my right, I followed the labyrinth. It was like being caught in a rip-tide. I could only just keep my balance as the energy raced me round and around to the core.

I stumbled into the sudden calm, then staggered again in an attempt to avoid trampling Ken.

Falling to my knees, I shook him. "Ken! Are you okay? Speak to me!"

There was no response.

"Ken?"

His breathing was faint but even; his pulse also faint and steady—like he was in a deep sleep. I couldn't wake him. Not knowing what else to do, I cradled his head in my arms and rocked, whispering his name constantly.

Around us, little energetic spirals of light streamed about like miniature galaxies; some so bright they hurt the eye, others so faint they almost weren't there. I don't know how long I rocked and whispered to him, "I love you, Ken. Don't leave me." Still he remained oblivious like some hero in a fairytale. He was too heavy for me to even attempt carrying or dragging him out.

The energy gathered speed. Dazzling lights obscured more and more of my bag and the balustrade. It all looked too dangerous to try leaving the calm centre. Were these flashes of light particles colliding? What exactly was going on? Shivering with fear, I clung to Ken.

The buzz, which had been all but subliminal, grew suddenly louder like an angry hive of bees on the attack. Fearing the worst, I buried my head in Ken's shoulder and sobbed. The buzz intensified. I couldn't think, my ears numbed.

***

Electricity prickled around and along us. One long heartbeat of anticipation later, the universe exploded into darkness so dense it had me choking, believing I would suffocate. I struggled to sit up, taking in large gulps of ozone-laden air. Slowly, the darkness receded, allowing my vision back. Ken had not moved at all.

The energy was dissipating, with only a few tendrils dancing in the BaGua. I shook Ken again. "Ken, please, wake up!" I was crying in shock. "Ken, please..." My tears fell onto his lips.

His mouth opened a fraction.

"Ken!"

His eyelids fluttered.

"Are you okay? Please, talk to me."

"Judy," he mumbled, his eyes opening.

"Are you hurt?"

His eyes were glowing; they all but dazzled me. Could he even see me?

His sudden smile was blissful. "Did you see it? Did you see the dragon?"

A new fear gripped me. The ordeal had driven him mad. "Ken," I began gently, "I don't know what exactly happened, but there was no dragon here."

He laughed. "Silly girl," he said with affection, sitting up.

Everything seemed to be more or less back to normal. The sunlight might have been duller than before, but fluffy clouds dotted the blue sky and warmth came gently along with the now playful breeze. I helped Ken up, still concerned. He was strangely happy; giddy even.

"I can't believe you missed it. It was right in front of you!" Ken kept saying, pleased like a little boy who knew a secret no-one else did.

"Maybe you need to see a doctor. Here, have some water." I handed him the bottle of spring water.

He took a long swig. "That's good!" he said, sitting down next to the bags. "Did you really not see it?"

"Yes," I sighed. "I always miss everything! Besides, I'm sure there was no dragon. Some kind of energy vortex, maybe... Are you sure you aren't hurt?" I touched his head gently, trying to feel if he hadn't concussed himself or worse.

He laughed again, holding my hand still in his. "Look at me."

He smiled. His eyes were mesmerizing, twin pools of silver luminous energy—like the BaGua...

"Judy, I'm the dragon you've been searching for."

I was a little scared, but I managed to keep my voice level. "Ken, you're cr...confused. We need to get you to a doctor."

His hands still held mine. They were hot, like a heat-pack. He drew me down, never breaking eye contact.

"You know it's true. I was hurt before. I didn't have all my powers. Now I do." *Watch!*

I heard him in my mind. He disappeared. On the warm sandstone, a miniature *Lung* with Ken's eyes stared back at me full of mischief.

I blinked in disbelief. "Ken?" I whispered.

The jewel-like creature flew up, whirring joyfully around me and tickled my ears with its tail. I giggled. Then he whizzed up high into the sky only to be lost to sight in a fraction of a second.

"Ken?"

You helped heal me.

His voice was in my mind again. I still couldn't see him. "But I did nothing! It was the BaGua."

He chuckled. *No, that was only part of it.* He swooped down again to land on his human feet, his face radiating joy. He took my hands again, raising me up to my feet. "Your love kept me centred when I needed it the most," he whispered, dropping a kiss on my hands. Then, "Told you we'd help each other with our quests!"

And he was suddenly back to being the man I knew instead of some fantastic mythical creature.

I didn't know what to say. I only knew I was an open book to him; more vulnerable emotionally, physically, spiritually, than I'd ever been to anyone else. He looked at me from under those eyelashes again. with affection.

I cleared my throat, then said, "Bit of a small dragon, aren't you?"

He laughed again, pulling me in for a hug. "I can get a lot bigger. Just didn't want to scare you."

"How big?" I mumbled into his shoulder, enveloped in a curious, comforting warmth; expecting him to say as big as a mountain, or as big as whale.

"As big as the world."

He said it so simply into my hair that I had no reason not to believe him. I shivered.

I pulled away. "How did it happen? How did you get injured? Can you really do all that weather stuff?" I was beginning to get excited, suddenly imagining myself becoming famous for bringing the story of an honest-to-goodness dragon to the whole world. Move over David Attenborough!

"Oh, no you don't!" he said, half teasing. I'm not ready for all that and neither is the world. Besides, I have a lot to do."

"Won't you tell me just a little bit more?" I gave him an imploring look.

He considered me intently before saying, "Okay. I was injured by another dragon—my nemesis, if you like. He'd thought he'd killed me, but I survived...and grew wiser. Now we'll have a reck-oning—and I mean to win this time." His eyes hardened.

"But you might get hurt!" The thought of losing Ken, dragon or not, appalled me.

"I won't!" he grinned wolfishly. "I have some-thing he doesn't."

"And what's that?"

He was silent for a moment. "It's a secret," he finally whispered with a strange, lopsided smile.

I glanced down blinking away tears, knowing this was him saying goodbye. "Now what?" I managed to say, "Are you going off to go save the world?"

"That's not dragon business. We have our own concerns. If the world gets saved as a consequence..."

I looked at him, trying to imprint his image in my brain. "Where will you go?"

"Everywhere. I have a lot of catching up to do."

I nodded, feeling the prickle of tears growing, my breath beginning to catch in my throat. "I guess this is goodbye then?"

"For now." He kissed me then, a light, breezy kiss. Then he was gone.

I stood a long time on that peaceful temple hilltop, wondering if I'd ever see him again; hoping that I would.

###

The BaGua first appeared on Sweek.com and was a finalist in the #sweeklove competition in February 2017. Originally written in 2010 when I lived in Yulin, it was one of the first stories I set in China. There's much from this story which influenced 'Situation No Win' and some of my later work.

SCIENCE FICTION/ FANTASY: LOCATION, AUSTRALIA

Hurtling across North-South dunes along East-West tracks could be fun.
But not today— not with three point five minutes left...

Hurtling on East-West tracks crossing North-South dunes, stuck beside a nesting backpacker with halitosis. Fairly good luck considering I could have been seated next to a green lizard guy, like the girl over on the left. Or...well, I could have been seated alongside me.

Hurtling across North-South dunes along East-West tracks could be fun. But not today—not with three point five minutes left.

I refused to contemplate it. I stared at Lizard Guy instead.

He stared back—for a full three minutes. Another minute and we'd fall in love, maybe.

Beanie adjusted, with a whole thirty seconds to spare, I headed down the swaying coach, intent on the restroom.

The restroom indicator switched from red to green. I was ready. So was Perseus.

He erupted out of the restroom, broken mirror held high.

Lucky I was looking down at his sandalled feet, with blue-black-nailed toes. Lucky, too, his movement was limited in the confined space. A kick to his knee, and throw into the corridor wall; problem solved—if only...

Athena's sword slashed my sleeve. I stepped back, stumbling over Perseus; no choice but to roll far back into the coach aisle.

Human shouts of alarm and frantic movement contrasted oddly with Lizard Guy's calm. No more observation time with both Perseus and Athena rushing me.

I itched to remove my beanie, my hair already wriggling for escape, and turn my adversaries into stone; but I couldn't risk it—not with so many innocents in danger.

I dropped into a crouch, wishing for my own sword, and that the two rows alongside me didn't hold panicky Seniors.

Perseus advanced, eyes gleaming with the realisation that my hair was hidden. Then I noticed Lizard Guy nodding at me and to the coach in general. All humans were stock-still. Only us so-called gods had movement. Lizard Guy glanced casually away.

I whipped off my beanie. My hair exploded, snaking out, turning Perseus and Athena into stone.

Sighing with relief and gratitude, I glanced at Lizard Guy. He was intently watching the dunes roll away. I shrugged, enjoying the freedom of my loose hair.

I rolled Athena back in the restroom, unsure how long Lizard Guy's stasis would last.

East-West tracks laid along North South dunes... Travelling at speed during the right con-stellation alignments makes opening a portal into any realm easy—perfect for Olympians staging a coup on Earth; perfect for Anunnaki travelling back home. A headache for Medusa, one of many protectors of the balance in realms.

Quickly, I kicked Athena and Perseus back home, then shut their portal. I resumed my seat, tucking my hair back into my beanie.

I stared at Lizard Guy as the coach stirred with confused passengers. He stared back with half a smile. We weren't friends, not by a long ways. Nor were we enemies, not yet.

A nod and a half-smile back at him. Satis-fied, I watched the last of the North-South dunes slide by.

This story, written for the prompt 'Medusa' in 2015, first appeared on S. Shane Thomas' Larc-scifi.com.

FANTASY: LOCATION, YOUR CHOICE

Love Like Water

But I had followed the instructions to the tee on Halloween,
the one night of the year where anything and everything
had to be possible. Then again, I'm not so sure that I'd gotten
the Latin pronunciation right. Was *amor* pronounced 'a more',
or 'a moray' or 'amow'...? I probably even got that wrong.

I stare up from the wet sand at the bright new moon, wishing it was a dark and stormy night. This bright cheerful, romantic path along the water doesn't suit my mood at all. I know I'm only depressed—only depressed, like it's such a small thing instead of a monster that steals your soul—because my spell hadn't worked.

Granted, I'm no witch. Granted, reading a book with a fake vellum cover, printed in China by a small-press English company, and following its instructions might not have been the best way to learn about spell-casting. But I had followed the instructions to the tee on Halloween, the one night of the year where anything and everything had to be possible. Then again, I'm not so sure that I'd gotten the Latin pronunciation right. Was *amor* pronounced 'a more', or 'a moray' or 'amow'...? I probably even got that wrong.

And here's me sitting with no boyfriend, again.

I'm tired of being alone: the gooseberry, the spare wheel. Tired of being mocked and pitied. Now even this darn cheery moon was getting in on it too. It's all too depressing. I haven't even bothered going to Kristoff's party this year. He's promised once again that there'll be a guy there for me. He promised that last year, and the year before, and the year before that... They always make an excuse and run off, especially the ones that look like my Ken doll. Why Kristoff thinks they're my type, I don't know...

The waves lap at my boots. I look down at them —traditional Docs, not the most comfortable, the only concession to my wannabe-Goth tendencies along with my black fingernails. It would be so easy to walk in, float off into nothingness... Dissolve this depression and loser-streak into something useful for the fishes.

I take a deep breath and look up for one last, calm sight of the moon.

There's a surfer rising out of the water, silhouetted in the silver light, jumping on his board, heading straight for me. I step back in alarm.

He reaches me in no time. I stumble back in shock. He looks exactly like my dream-guy: no Ken, but with his long sun-bleached locks around a strong, rugged face; tribal tattoos covering his arm and flowing towards his heart; a multi-cultural Adonis. His eyes are dark, and so deep a whole universe or two could be hiding in them.

"You've asked me to come find you, now I'm

here." His lips move—no sound, but I hear his smooth, low voice in my mind.

I feel so strongly drawn to him, like my Gran's fridge magnets to an industrial electro-magnet. I stare at him open-mouthed. I manage to choke out, "Who are you?"

"I am the one you called to. I am your man."

I open and close my mouth. There's so much I want to ask him, so many questions. What did he mean I called to him? Unless... "My spell last year!"

"Yes," he smiles with pearly white teeth. "You came here last year when the moon was hidden by rain. You called to me using the language of your ancestors. You told me you were ready. Remember?"

I remember. I don't know exactly what those Latin words translate into, only that they had been a love spell for your soulmate. Maybe some of me had leaked into it, the message to the spirits and worlds open to my spell last Halloween.

"Oh." And, because I'm only human, "What took you so long?"

He laughs, a deep chuckle that makes the stars twinkle a little brighter. "I had errands to run and things to attend to. My father keeps me busy."

I struggle to speak again, my heart thumping harder than usual. My head so light I feel I'm going to fly off with the butterflies in my tummy. "Who... Who exactly are you?"

"I am Manannan, Son of Mac Lir, Prince of the Seas."

"But..." How could such a man, such a god, want me to be his?

His face falls. "Will you not come with me then? Will you not be my woman? Is this not what you wanted?"

"Yes! No! I mean...things are moving a bit fast."

He smiles again. "That is the way of love—like water, ebbing and flowing. Would you build walls and dams to slow it unnaturally?"

He's so heartbreakingly beautiful that I hear myself saying, "No."

"Then it's decided," he says, and takes my hand.

I float on a wave of euphoria along the path of the moon, surrounded by his love.

***

They find me the next morning lying on the sand.

"Tracy! Tracy!" calls Kristoff, sharp concern in his voice.

I stir reluctantly, more comfortable than in my own bed.

"What happened?" demands Kristoff, looking down at me, surrounded by Zombies and slinky witches stinking of beer and rum. "You're soaking wet. Quick, let's get her warm." He shrugs off his jacket.

"I'm fine," I smile. "He came for me. And he'll be back next year."

"What are you talking about?"

"She's out of it, dude," adds a Zombie.

My smile is still glowing with love. "He'll be back next Halloween, the one night of the year he's off duty and the worlds lie close enough to surf across."

I sit up and stare across the pink waters of the new dawn. "Next year," I tell Kristoff, "I have a real date!"

The monster of depression has dissolved in the seas of my love.

"What's this?" Kristoff gingerly fingers a bracelet of silvery green-blue metal around my wrist.

I laugh. It has to be from Manannan. I put it to my ear, and hear his chuckle.

###

Written in 2015 for a Halloween prompt, this story first appeared on my blog www.leennanaidoo.word-press.com

SCIENCE FICTION: LOCATION, USA

PLay With ELFs

...For I shall always love you **as even now
the ELFs shall save you!**

From the personal correspondence of Moshin Hed-bange, inventor of the Hear-It-Tru Musical Headset Range and the Beats off Dissonance health system, who disappeared mysteriously on May, 5th 2018.

***

Letter to Thomas Eldrin Dornish, best friend and confidante

May 1st, 2018

Hey Tommy

I need a little favour. A little one, I promise, not like the last one. And yes, I'll promise I shall never again pick on the size and shape of your bald dome, even though its… Okay, I promise! See, I'm keeping it already!

So here's the deal. I need you to pass on this sealed letter to Kimmi.

I know it's a little strange and all, seeing how you two are together now, but I swear on both my eardrums that it is most, *most* urgent to get this to her. And you know she's not talking to me after our last little meeting.

And I swear to you that I'm not trying to win

her back again. No, this little note is all about work and the future. And since she was such a big part of all the initial research on Hear-It-Tru and then Beats Off Dissonance...You see what I'm getting at, don't you, Tommy?

No matter what it seems like, it's all about what you warned me about back in 2013, and well, you were right about Musseller. So darn right. And...

Just get that note to Kimmi please. It's very private and very important. And whatever Kimmi decides to do, please support her in it, 'cos god knows I can't.

Your buddy, always

Moshin

***

Letter to Kimberley Olssen, lab assistant at GLARRU

May 1st, 2018

My dearest Kimmi

The truth, my love. I know you hate my poems, but please, **hear me out**, even if **secretly** you detest me.

They say, **no heart beats** truer 'cos of little ones like **mines!**

Even **my inventions, serve as obscurations** and scorched the truth.

Now that **I'm compelled to beat all drums of those who ear me**,

I must **play with ELFs** in order **to save thee**...

Waves of fear, I have to commit, have eroded my **terrible deeds** from my memory.

I beg you, please, please, forgive me.

My **pulsing** needs **resonates** with the **death of all** my **know** fears of the **future** with you!

Please, please, don't forget all the times I **measured** your **skulls**, and the **violently** expressed emotions which **exploded the bodies** we had.

Now you must save all I was and ever shall be.

Destroy the beats of dissonance, destroy all that we measured before. Destroy all that you hate, **the music** of your mate...

Cancel all that **out.**

For I shall always love you as even now **the ELFs shall save you!**

All my love and fervent wishes

Moshin

***

Email to Alfred J Musseller, CEO of Musical Endeavours and CEO of Global Armoury R-Us.

May 2nd, 2018

Musseller

I must again insist that you cease production of the Dissonator 2.1.

Even you must see the obvious. Unleashing a machine which measures the resonance of every structure in sight and then releases an electro-magnetic wave of equal dissonance is simply monstrous, and not at all what we discussed when I sold you the patents to the Hear-It-Tru system.

I should never have believed you when you said that you were oh-so eager to support my dream of people being able to record their voices as they hear them in their heads.

I should never have believed you when you said that you were oh-so eager to ensure that music be heard exactly as the musician intended, and not as listeners' individual skulls distorted the rhythms...

I should never have believed you when you said

the next step would be applying all that knowledge to electromagnetic waves to enhance sound equipment...

You are a...a... Words fail me, so play the media file attached.

I can't let you do it, Musseller.

I won't let you sell those skull resonance and dissonance generating algorithms to the military. And I won't let you get away with destroying another town like Perfectionville, much less the whole of civilisation as we know it. Not with my inventions!

I was mad to trust you, and now I'm just mad.

So know this:

Any attempt to activate the Dissonator 2.1 will result in its self-destruction.

Any attempt to tamper with the Dissonator 2.1, the Dissonator, 1.1 and the Beats Off Dissonance Apps will result in their destruction.

And yours, I might add.

That's right. They are all rigged to take out exactly 2.25808 square kilometres, emitting a mixedtape of sound and electro-magnetic frequencies to resonate with everything and everyone in the GLARRU installation. You will have realised by now that 2.25808 kilometres is the distance from your office to GLARRU's main gate.

You will have also realised that I've uploaded your skull's resonant/dissonance tones onto your laptop.

You aren't wriggling out of this one, Musseller, not like you did in Perfectionville.

So, I must insist, for your own health and all of your employees, DO NOT ATTEMPT TO ACTIVATE OR TAMPER WITH MY INVENTIONS.

Yours in good health, not!

Moshin Hedbange

***

From the files of investigative journalist Caroline MacAllister Dubbin, who won the Pulitzer prize for her exposure of the events surrounding the then inexplicably sudden total destruction of Perfectionville, New Mexico, and the demise and unheralded destruction of Global Armoury R-Us holdings worldwide.

Her interview with sole surviving GLARRU employee, Kimberley Olssen, won MacAllister a People's Choice Award in 2019. She is still searching for inventor Moshin Hedbange in the hopes of finding the conclusion to this intriguing story.

FANTASY: SOMETIME, SOMEWHERE...

Substitute Ice-cream

The parlour was busy. In front of him stood a witch, her face green,
her steeple hat immaculate.
"You know," Norbet couldn't help himself. "Halloween's not for another eight months."
She turned, revealing a hideous squint almost as good as his aunt Betty's.
"Eye of Newt, know whereabouts I might find some, sonny?"

Norbet's bewildered expression clouded his handsome face. The manual, sorry—grimoire, demanded Eye Of Newt which didn't exist since the last enviro disaster. And Bat's Blood? Would blood from a baseball bat count? Conjuring up a date for Valentines Day had to be simpler, or was this his Mum being tricky? He decided ice-cream was needed.

The parlour was busy. In front of him stood a witch, her face green, her steeple hat immaculate.

"You know," Norbet couldn't help himself, "Halloween's not for another eight months."

She turned, revealing a hideous squint almost as good as his aunt Betty's. "Eye of Newt, know whereabouts I might find some, sonny?"

"Not in here!" said Norbet with a smile. "Looking for some myself. Don't know how I'm going to find Bat's Blood too."

She gazed right through him, her practised squint forgotten, the glamour of years dropping off her. "I'm Tilda. Third year of working this bloody spell. It's hellish, the results I've gotten with substitute ingredients. Why are you working it? Gorgeous guy like you should have all the girls queueing up."

Norbet blushed. "My mum's the Grand Witch."

"The one who—?"

"Yes," said Norbeth, wishing Tilda wouldn't spell it out.

Tilda's smile transformed her into the most beautiful girl Norbet had ever seen.

"Always wanted to meet her."

Norbeth knew fate when he met it. "Would you be my Valentine? Just for the Dance?"

Tilda beamed. "I'd love to."

Norbet smiled. Ice-cream won as a substitute every time.

###

This story first appeared on Sweek.com

SCIENCE FICTION: LOCATION, AUSTRALIA (MAYBE, MAYBE NOT)

A Good Record

Transcript from the
Voice-recorder of Prof Len S Clare

...Such beautiful eyes! I swear they see right through me—right through my soul
and all that mushy stuff. Now where's that screwdriver?
And she wants to pay me for the commission!
Unbelievable!
But now that I think about it, my VL Flash Imager is just perfect for a cryptozoologist!

Transcript from the Voice Recorder of Prof. Len S. Clere—October 27th

Who'd have thought there would be such an application for my Violet Light Flash Imager! Or that Stacy Stevens would be the one to contact me! All those years of wishing I could speak to her at the university canteen, only to have her speak to me over the... (*sound of things moving around the counter masks some words*)...after she read my paper on the university site. She even ignored all those disparaging remarks from Pudding Face! Who would have thought!

(*Rapid footsteps and the clang of small metal objects clashing together*). Note to self: must clean up before she visits tomorrow.

(*Sound of body tripping and falling heavily*). Oof! What the... Oh! My old Brownie! That's where it got to. It will be just perfect. Just perfect! The right size, and simple enough to convert; or maybe just disassemble the flash and stick it onto a digital cam. Yes, much better idea, much more compact.

(*indistinct muttering along with sounds of heavy body picking itself up*).

Such beautiful eyes! I swear they see right

through me—right through my soul and all that mushy stuff. Now where's that screwdriver? And she wants to pay me for the commission! Unbelievable! But now that I think about it, my VL Flash Imager is just perfect for a cryptozoologist! Oww! (*Indistinct swearing*). Band-aid. Band-aid. Ah, there they are. Waterproof too! What luck! Although when she looks at me, I just want to melt away or hide...

(*A second of silence*)

Hide! Hide! What if the VL Flash is not powerful enough to penetrate a creature's hide? After all, a cryptozoologist will want as much data as possible.

Note to self: Test immediately on various hides and stuff—fur, crocodile, tortoiseshell. Her hairgrip was tortoiseshell—fake I hope... Note to self: Acquire *real* tortoiseshell and hides, not the fake stuff. (*sound of footsteps rapidly pacing a small space*) Where to get them at such short notice? Where to get them? Biology Department? Cultural Studies department...Museum! Natural Science Museum. Perfect! Just perfect! (*footsteps stop*).

I'll take the New Compact Digital VL Flash

Imager over for a test run. Not quite field conditions for a cryptozoologist, but, you never know what you're going to run into at a museum these days. After all, that's where I first ran into Stacy all those years ago in second year, and knocked her down along with that Orca skeleton. Thank goodness she never ever found out that was me. What a day that was—I was so excited...!

(*Sudden silence, then a rush of footsteps*)

Excited dimers! Excited dimers! I still have to prep the Excimer Lamp materials! Fill the flash with halogen and stuff! And this time I must keep a good record! Are you on recorder? (*sound of tapping on plastic surface and windy sounds over the mic*). Very good, excellent. Perfect. There'll be an audio record this time. I'm sure there's enough memory on the card. I only just changed it before Stacy's visit... And... Where was I? Oh, yes. Excimer Lamp to be converted in flashbulb. No prob. All I have to—

(*End of file*)

***

Transcript from the Voice-recorder of Prof Len S Clere—October 28th

File 1

Testing testing. *(Brief silence, then sounds of fumbling. Abrupt end of file).*

File 2

Testing testing. Oh, never mind. Let's see if this works. *(click and whirr of servo).* Oh my goodness! It doesn't work! That triceratops skeleton looks just the same. *(Sounds of fumbling).* Let's just try this again and look alive this time.

(two seconds of silence)

Alive! Alive this time! But of course! This will only work on live subjects. How can you see the alternate state of something if it's dead. If it lacks charge! *(Sound of palm slapping into forehead or similar)* What a doofus! *(Sounds of sudden intense activity)* I'll try this at the zoo. Lots of live animals and stuff there. People too.

(End of file).

***

Transcript from the voice-recorder of Prof. Len S. Clere—October 28th.

File 3

...fragile like that butterfly's wings. Don't know

how Stacy survives all those excursions into jungles and...(*speech obscured by sounds of camera being set up*). Ah, there we go. The butterfly enclosure. Stay still, little butter...Perfect. Just perfect! It's a little fuzzy, but the cocoon is clear enough, superimposed over the butterfly like that. Never before realized that the caterpillar is still there, just with wings...

(A *second of silence*)

Guess Stacy will be winging away off to some far-off place once she's got the VL Cam with her. Who am I kidding? She'll be winging away even without it. Mason says she's off to Aussie land. Don't know...(*mumbling obscured by whirring of servo*).

Oh! I'm so sorry, sir! I didn't mean... Here let me help you up. I'm so...(*babble of voices, one low and angry*)...never happen again, I *assure* you. And I'll thank you to let go my shirt now.

(*Muffled question*)

Yes, I am recording this for strictly scientific purposes. And... Oh no! Please! It's a very rare piece of equip—. (*Sounds of breaking equipment,*

angry growling possibly human, and whimpering pro-
tests).

***

**Transcript from the Voice-recorder of Prof Len
S Clere—October 28th**

File 4

...will be pleased, I'm sure. Maybe she'll even
invite me on her next expedition! Though I don't
know why that angry man has that short tail
superimposed on his... Oh! I know! I'll show it to
Stacy! It will be good for a laugh at least! Maybe
I could even convince her he was a were-bear! A
were-bear! (*gales of laughter*). A *were*...oh yes. I'll
definitely show it to her along with the butterfly. And personally demonstrate to her how to use
the flash.

(*moment of silence*)

Flash it all! Why did that tail-guy have to destroy that flashbulb and camera. Now, I'll have to
start from scratch. (*Sounds of dispirited tinkering*).
At least there's still the old Brownie collection in
the attic. But only eighteen more hours before
Stacy's expecting her...

(*two seconds of silence*)

Eighteen more hours! I can't disappoint her! Excimers, flash! They all have to be ready to demonstrate, otherwise I'll never have this good a chance to...(*mumbling and sounds of items moving around counter*)...get a proper record this time! I know I changed the memory card just this morning! So here—

(*end of file*)

Also written for a mad scientist prompt, this is the first publication of this story which refers to Stacy, the cryptozoologist. Look for her adventure in Aussie-land in **The Walpole Were**.

SCIENCE FICTION: LOCATION, SOMEWHERE ON EARTH...

What the Boy Didn't Know

The old man lowered the sail as he reached his spot, then anchored.
Beneath him a shoal swam.
He cast his line and settled comfortably in his seat,
admiring the translucent beauty of the water.

The old man was fond of the boy but was glad he didn't have to keep up the pretence of fishing any more. He felt almost guilty about the way his failure to catch fish had sealed his reputation. No-one would ever go fishing with him again, and that was just dandy. The last thing he needed on his last earthly days was to be distracted by relationships.

The old man lowered the sail as he reached his spot, then anchored. Beneath him a shoal swam. He cast his line and settled comfortably in his seat, admiring the translucent beauty of the water.

With a solar storm approaching, it took a little longer than usual for his rod to tune in and the transmission to begin. Instantly, the upset shoal scattered. The old man smiled, thinking about the boy and villagers.

The planet's network linked in easily. Judging from the strength of the transmission tingling through his fingertips, he knew this upload was a quite a big one. More species endangered, more tracts of land degraded...Why did they even bother?

The old man, not of this Earth but in love

with it, knew the answer: for the boy and those like him.

###

Written for the prompt 'The Old Man and The Sea', this is the first publication of this story

SCIENCE FICTION: LOCATION, AN ASTEROID IN SPACE

SOULS PROVIDER

Coru guessed the sender was a bored ore-driver.
Who else would torment the loneliest of celestial residents?

Be my Valentine.

The display was superimposed across Coru's domed-view of the galaxy. Two Valentines ago, the message had read: *Meet me for dinner?* Strange, with her the only being on Asteroid SOLE PROVIDER. Besides, matchmakers insisted soulmates weren't found in space.

Coru guessed the sender was a bored ore-driver. Who else would torment the loneliest of celestial residents?

Wishing she wasn't condemned by incompatibility, she erased the message and went back to core analyses with only ancient Bublè songs for company.

Eight hours later, she was back at the dome, flummoxed. The craft approaching, with its stingray profile, indicated Arccidian origin.

Coru Spanspek, I await your answer, flickered across the dome.

Her heart froze. The keeper on Asteroid Base One had come to a mysterious and bloody end after an inept informal meeting...

But she had always longed for a Valentine.

Coru took a deep breath, and sent back: *I'd be honoured.*

Soon, Coru stood biting her lip and with her fists clenched as the airlock swirled open.

Perfumed roses greeted her first, framed by a slim humanoid torso. A long-fingered hand offered her an exquisite box. Her mouth watered at the smell of luxury—chocolate!

Coru?

His eyes like miniature sparkling galaxies were smiling, though his mouth did not.

I've admired you for long and wish for a deeper relationship.

Coru's heart skipped at his sincerity. Love infused her from his being. She beamed at him. Her soul-mate had finally found her.

###

This story first appeared on Sweek.com

FANTASY: LOCATION, OUT IN THE COUNTRY

Hawk-Eyed

We don't call ourselves hawks for nothing.

About that pile of clothes you found on the ground? They were mine. But it's not what you think.

Yes, I did see Lucy last night. I also saw you.

You see, Lucy and I are a team—The Hawks; setting rights to wrong.

So while you sat there laughing in relief, happy that you could run into Steve's arm's guilt-free, I watched you from the tree. We don't call ourselves hawks for nothing.

Be seeing you. Don't be surprised if more lambs disappear this season, or if field animals fall onto your windscreen. It's just my way of saying hi.

###

This story first appeared on Sweek.com

FANTASY: LOCATION, WESTERN AUSTRALIA (WHERE ELSE?)

CONFESSIONS OF A SHAPE-SHIFTER:
All Aussie Family

How was I to know she'd stand about laughing, or find it endearing?
I know people think we're cute, but it's no laughing matter
not after growing up outside Perth, with farmers gunning for you.

Should have told Stacy first thing, with her being a cryptozoologist an' all. It's just that...I've never had to tell anyone else before.

Had enough badgering about my legs growing up; enough snide remarks on how I jumped, and my dancing like Yahoo Serious...

How was I to know she'd stand about laughing, or find it endearing? I know people think we're cute, but it's no laughing matter—not after growing up outside Perth, with farmers gunning for you.

Still, gotta tell her there's not just roos in the family, but Salties too. Hope she's just as delighted then.

###

This story first appeared on Sweek.com, and yep. It might be related to The Walpole Were too :-)

SCIENCE FICTION: LOCATION, SOME FUTURE CITY

Switch Twitch

With a pocket full of gold, and the world-jumping gadget,
I could Switch Twitch my life, not just a pocket.
The multiverse was my oyster.
I'd be stupid not to search for the pearl.

I'd gotten it off some old guy with shifty, suspicious eyes and a wallet full of gold and formulas. I knew it had to be something special.

I'd studied some before realising it wasn't going to feed me, while sleight of hand could. Besides, I'd swotted for years and taken the test to become a world-jumping pilot before they told me I couldn't qualify because my folks didn't have the money for the 'application'. With a pocket full of gold, and the world-jumping gadget, I could Switch Twitch my life, not just a pocket. The multiverse was my oyster. I'd be stupid not to search for the pearl.

Once I'd figured out the sequence this little bracelet used, I jumped just a little way—just to familiarise myself with things.

There was a hint of nausea when I stepped right into the parallel world two strings away—not so much the switch as much as the air quality. Crowded city, stinky air with thick particles. I might well have jumped in time to my string's Industrial Revolution. No pearls here. I ducked into an alley and switch twitched with a smile at the home-boy who was reaching for his gun.

I jumped further this time, hoping to get better air, and better-looking people. My old textbooks had said that the third world Jonas Kirby had jumped to during his testing phase had been pure hell, while the fifth had been pure heaven. That's where he'd eventually disappeared to, hiding the co-ords so none could follow him. I'd have done the same if the Feds had been after me too.

***

The world seven strings away from my former home was too green. Green air, but breathable. Green people with shocked expressions. Blue cops with puce faces pursuing. Too hard to Switch here. I jumped strings while running—an absolute no-no in anyone's textbook.

I found out why in the thirteen world from my home string. Velocities don't match. I ran straight through a stone wall and into a barn. Bucolic looking world—may well have been a pearl. I'm a city boy at heart. Even those four-horned hairy cows could see it. Too hairy for me. I waved at the farmer's wife screaming, "Witch! Witch!" and the farmhands running over with pitchforks. Pity. The air was so pure...

I kinda liked the twentieth world, but the dragons didn't like me; and the twenty-fifth? Too lonely with it's whole dystopian filmset look. The thirty-first world? Heavy, man—gravity ruled with an iron-fist. I almost didn't make it out of that one.

I got to tell you, I was getting desperate now. A pocket full of gold and a gidget to Switch Twitch anywhere in an infinite number of worlds, and I still get stuck with the duds. I had to turn the lemons into lemonade, as my mum used to say.

***

It was the fifty-third world that decided me. Nothing but tardigrades munching or keening, and hydras free-wheeling all over the place. I'd came, I'd seen, I jumped to too many conclusions. It was time to go back home.

I almost didn't make it back. There was this one string. So beautiful and pristine—and this one girl... I stayed two years and turned my pocketful into a disgusting fortune with one of those formulas. But... No matter how hard I tried, I just couldn't get used to the purple sky and lighter gravity. There's no place like home, as they say.

***

Home felt strange at first. I felt...different, too. I stood for a few moments, taking everything in— the milling people, the heavy air, the haves and the have-nots with barely concealed hostility...

Someone bumped into me, so I stepped to the side against a store, and felt for the gidget one last time, to say goodbye like.

It wasn't on my wrist. I checked my pocket. Empty.

I should have guessed. Slowly, I turned to look at the store window. There reflected, like my future, stood I—an old man with shifty, suspicious eyes.

I grinned at myself savagely. There's no place like home.

###

This story first appeared online in Quantum Shorts 2015, and was not placed.

SCIENCE FICTION: LOCATION, IN A LAB SOMEWHERE (TODAY, OR MAYBE YESTERDAY)

SPLIT INfinite

There was just no talking Archer out of his crazy theories.
Everyone wanted to figure out dark matter,
and he severely doubted it would be his crazed colleague
with his super-freezing-a-neutrino idea.

"I just need to split a neutrino. That will gener-ate dark matter. I'm sure of it!" Archer took a bite of his ham and pickle sandwich.

"Yeah, right. You keep reaching for the im-possible." Madurah brought a forkful of pasta to his mouth, then added, "You know it's impossible right? Ain't nothing smaller than a neutrino."

"That we know of." Archer was always ready to defend his favourite theory. "That's what they said about the atom, and then quarks...We just don't have the means to detect anything smaller just now. Doesn't mean it's not there."

Madurah shook his head. There was just no talking Archer out of his crazy theories. Everyone wanted to figure out dark matter, and he severely doubted it would be his crazed colleague with his super-freezing-a-neutrino idea. He just hoped Archer wouldn't blow up the lab again. He needed it in pristine shape for his mini-collider test; his tenure depended on it.

***

Archer worked late into that night. Security guards confirmed having last seen him around 11:30pm. At about 1:13am, a giant power surge swept through the labs and raced across town, shorting everything in its path. Wild electricity arced for miles out of the harbour, anchored by the stevedore cranes.

Madurah rushed out to the labs, instinct telling him Archer had produced another calamity he would have to clean up. Sure enough, rescue services had the complex sealed off. There was no sign of Archer. All the ambulances stood empty.

***

The next morning, Madurah found the whole department standing outside what was left of the lab Archer and he had shared.

"Inexplicable. Truly inexplicable!" Professor Ellison sounded awed instead of all knowing, for once. "Not a single human casualty, and now this!"

Madurah pushed his way forward to get a better look at 'this'. A dark cloud engulfed part of the passage. It absorbed most of the fluorescent light, leaving the lab entrance in impenetrable darkness.

Madurah gaped. Surely, it couldn't be! Surely Archer hadn't...

He turned abruptly to his colleagues. "No casualties, you said. Where's Archer? The hospital?"

Some of the staff shifted uncomfortably. Others looked keenly between Madurah and Ellison.

"I honestly don't know, Madurah." Most of Ellison's attention was on the dark cloud swirling around the lab entrance. "He called in just a few minutes ago to say he's fine."

Madurah frowned, but not for long.

A phone began ringing. Dr Govender took the call. Almost at once, she called out, "It's for Madurah."

Madurah felt sick. What had Archer gotten him into this time? Slowly, he picked up the receiver from the desk where Govender had set it. "Hello, Madurah here."

Archer's voice was unmistakable. "Hey man, you'll never believe it! I did it! I split the neutrino. But you were right; there's no dark matter produced."

Madurah choked, then cleared his throat. "You sure, man? 'Cos there's something dark and foggy around the lab; no light getting through. I reckon that could be your dark matter. Where are you anyway? Come over here and see it."

Archer's chuckle was warm, and happier than Madurah had ever heard him. "No need, I'm already there. Can't see the dark cloud though. Must be in a lower energy state."

"Hey, man. Quit fooling around!" Madurah glanced quickly at the empty office, and through the glass window giving onto the crowded corridor. "I know you're not here. I'd see you otherwise."

"Oh, but I am." Archer chuckled softly. "There's been an amazing result from my experiment—completely unpredicted, but one that makes wonderful sense when you see what I now see..."

A chill passed through Madurah. "Really, what's that?"

There was a silence from Archer, as if he was trying to find a good description. Eventually, he said, "You know when your mum told you angels could be everywhere at once? Well, I can too. I am here, there and everywhere—all at once! Do you know what this means?"

Madurah stood open-mouthed. Was he talking to a ghost or an angel?

"It means, when I split the neutrino, it shot me into such a high energy state that I'm...I'm pure energy! No particle or wave, but pure energy in a form we've never perceived before! And so is everything around me, man. It's so beautiful! So peaceful, so absolutely perfect!"

Madurah trembled. He knew Archer well enough to know what was coming next.

"But," went Archer in that way he had, "I'm going to need someone to help me with further experiments. I could do things on my level and you can verify them, and vice versa. There's so much to document! Did you know that light is just clumps of energy, and when it's unravelled...Oh, man! Madurah? You there?"

Madurah lay on the floor, hyperventilating. There had to be a rational explanation for this phone call. Archer was just playing some elaborate joke, like that fiasco last year. There was no way what Archer said was true. No way at all.

From his vantage point on the floor, he could see the swirl and eddying of the dark fog. A strange sensation reached his left ear.

Archer said distinctly, "Ah, I see you now. I know it's all a bit of a shock, but think of the possibilities, man. Think of the possibilities!"

Madurah thought about all the opportunities he'd missed through the years, the smirks on his colleagues faces when they heard he was sharing a lab with Archer... And he smiled. Limitless possibilities equals infinite opportunities—in every plane's speak.

And edited version of this story appeared online on Quantum Shorts 2015 (unplaced), but I prefer this unedited version.

FANTASY: LOCATION, SCOTLAND

OUT OF BRAMBLES

A creative sabbatical
to write my new cookbook made this
old cottage in Scotland my temporary home.
It was a tad lonely...and spooky.

"Bubble, bubble, taste of sambals," I intoned, slightly high on chocolate wine. "Let my love climb out of brambles." I added the bramble jelly wondering where on earth that had come from.

Shrugging, I stirred my Halloween dinner. Tree branches tapped the window. I shivered. I'd never been a fan of October squalls. Time for my sweater.

My first Halloween alone.

A creative sabbatical to write my new cookbook made this old cottage in Scotland my temporary home. It was a tad lonely...and spooky. The tapping at the window increased with the gusty wind.

I turned on the radio. "...tale, by The Erskine Storytelling Association."

I sipped my wine, hoping the story would be good."

"It was a dark and stormy night..."

I groaned, too comfortable in my chair to move just yet.

"...a ghostly knock on the door," went the narrator.

How could a knock on the door be 'ghostly'? Soft, tentative, loud, unexpected, maybe...

I stood up. The pot needed a stir.

"You called for me, and now I have come," rasped the radio.

I stopped. That sounded different, not like the narrator at all. I turned off the radio, and plugged in my flash-drive. The distinctive sounds of The Cure merged nicely with the weather.

I opened the pot, breathing in deeply. I could almost taste the divine sweet and sour notes already.

Smiling, I closed the pot and turned around.

"You called for me, and now I have come!"

I stared into the light-grey eyes of the man standing in my kitchen. His haggard, annoyed face reminded me of a man pulled out of bed for a trifle. He was handsome in a ragged way, with a dark ponytail and simple clothes.

"What will you have me do, Mistress?"

"I beg your pardon!" I wasn't anybody's mistress, and I never meant to be. What was this stranger, a man twice as heavy and tall as me, doing in my rented kitchen—full of my newest, most secret recipes?

"Who are you? Who sent you? Have you come

to steal my recipes?" I inched towards the sink where a sharp knife and a frying pan lay.

"I am the Dark Man of Erskine. You have called and I have come, Mistress. I know nothing of recipes." His eyes slanted towards the pot. "That smells delicious. It is surely more than haggis and neeps you cook there."

My heart softened. He must have been passing in the storm, and smelt the cooking. He looked half-starved anyway. Maybe all he wanted was a hot meal.

"It's...." I hadn't named the dish yet; hadn't even tasted it. And here was a man with an empty stomach. "...something new. No haggis and neeps; but if you'd like, pull up a chair and I'll get you a bowl and a glass of wine."

He looked surprised. "Mistress, are you sure that is what you want of me?"

"I don't want anything of you, and stop calling me Mistress!" I said, spooning the hearty stew into two bowls. "But, you can tell me what you think of this." I placed a steaming bowl on the kitchen table.

He raised an eyebrow. "Are you sure?"

"Quite sure," I insisted, pouring him some chocolate wine—the only wine I had left.

"I thank you, Mis...Ma'am." He sat down and picked up a spoon.

I joined him, my bowl opposite his. He took a spoonful, the smell of damp earth accompanying the scent of my cooking. What an odd man!

I tasted the stew. It was good, but...

"This is good!" He had finished his serving.

He looked at the pot. I obliged, filling up his bowl again.

"Do you like the bramble in it?" I asked.

He smiled. "Indeed I do. It is my favourite! Especially with the rose tea!"

I was impressed. I had added some rose tea. What a fine palate! "Who are you?" I was still confused. "Are you from around here?"

He put down his spoon, satisfied, and turned his attention to the wine.

"You are a fine cook, ma'am. The best I've met in years, so I shall be truthful with you. I am the Dark Man of Erskine, once the Lord Erskine's wayward son, but now a spirit to be called upon by a mistress on Halloween—"

"But!" I protested. "I was cooking! I wasn't..." Then it struck me.

He was smiling at me, a curious, amused smile.

"Are you...?" I couldn't say it. It was too preposterous! So I tried, "Just how old are you?"

His smile grew sad. "I am two-hundred-and-twenty-seven years old, by most reckoning." Then he brightened up. "And that was the best meal I have had in one-hundred-and-ninety years! So, I shall not take you with me."

I looked askance at him.

He explained. "When a mistress calls the Dark Lord of Erskine, she may have him do as she pleases for that Halloween. Then she must accompany him back to his resting place."

I shivered again. It was hard not to believe him.

He continued. "Your meal has brought me peace and well-being, something I have not experienced since childhood. Two more such meals, and my lonely soul shall gain peace. Will you help me, ma'am?"

I had to know, "How did you...die?"

"I was poisoned by my mistress."

I sat speechless. The wind howled, then died down to a whisper.

"Will you cook for me—just two more meals to set my soul free?"

How could I not? "Well, I do need a taster for my newest recipes. And with taste-buds like yours…"

His smiled beatifically. "We are agreed?"

I smiled back. "If you do the dishes."

He laughed, nodding.

My spookiest Halloween, but by far the most productive. Besides, no gourmet goes to hell from my kitchen.

###

This story, my first ever sale at a professional rate, appeared in Cosmic Roots and Eldritch Shores in 2016, editor Fran Eisemann, illustrations by

SCIENCE FICTION: LOCATION, AT A LITTLE-KNOWN CONVENTION

On Conveying Private Material and Persons in the Solar System

While this was the way in the past, it is not the way of the future, or mine anyway.
My calculations and experiments have shown me the remarkably simple,
and massively cost-saving, way of conducting all my equipment and supplies
into space and onto Mars utilitising a simple and old-fashioned method—balloons!
These balloons are, naturally, augmented by a few of my new and old inventions.

By Prof M.A De Bruin (as told to Leenna Naidoo)

I've often been told that it is impossible for a private concern, much less a private individual, to set up a safe, secure, and self-sustaining enterprise on the Red Planet. Some have even taken my so-called obsession with Mars—and indeed, settling there—as a sign of mental illness.

For this, I must thank those individuals who had me consigned to the Institute for three years; for it was there that I was forced to relax my mind, allowed to experiment with both sound and un-sound ideas, and eventually to realise how exceed-ingly simple it would be to achieve my dream: my own self-sustaining legacy for the future of Mars!

Let me address the first concern of most schol-ars and engineers about setting up a base on Mars, or even the Moon: the cost of escaping Earth's atmosphere.

It takes all that fuel (rocket fuel) to propel any-thing into our atmosphere and to achieve escape velocity. All one hears is: We must expend x amount of exorbitantly expensive fuel in order to create x amount of thrust for x amount of mass to reach escape velocity and then its ultimate des-tination.

While this was the way in the past, it is not the way of the future, or mine anyway.

My calculations and experiments have shown me the remarkably simple, and massively cost-saving, way of conducting all my equipment and supplies into space and onto Mars, utilising a simple and old-fashioned method—balloons! These balloons are, naturally, augmented by a few of my new and old inventions.

****

My calculations showed that the proper use of a fleet of helium balloons will elevate x amount of mass to a height of over 20,000 feet and thus reduce the amount of fuel used by at least 20% as compared to conventional methods!

At this height, my method calls for some ingenuity, if I say so myself, in order to propel my load into space and beyond. Here is where meteorology comes into play.

As the balloon mass glides across the skies, prior careful preparations will ensure that the balloons are near the upward draft of a large supercell storm! This upward draft will draw the balloons swiftly and effortlessly higher into the troposphere whilst simultaneously charging my patented plasma batteries, which are used for navigation and emergency power once out of Earth's atmosphere. At the same time, of course, the higher pressures within the weather system will be working on the second stage propulsion device —one which is filled with compressed gunpowder. At the optimum pressure, a tiny lightning rod will be extended by each load cylinder attached to individual balloons. Nature will oblige in igniting the gunpowder, gravity will be stunned and escape velocity of the payload will be achieved. Nothing could be simpler!

***

I shall now move onto the next concern of my peers: cost of propulsion to the destination.

As my work is centred primarily on Mars, that is the destination I shall use in my example.

My individual payloads, containing optimum masses of no more than 25 kilograms, are now safely out of Earth's atmosphere and in orbit. This is where my newest invention, the Sunscreemer as I like to call it (forgive me my little joke), comes into its own. The Sunscreemer, using a system of revolutionary solar panels and compressed gunpowder, will lock into the most direct, obstacle-free course to Mars (or any other programmed destination) and, at the optimum time, it will launch the 25 kilogram payload to its destination. I have achieved accuracies of within 1 kilometre of my target thus far, and am sure that with just a little more tinkering, I shall achieve accuracy of within 25 meters of the target.

These methods, accurate and cheap as they are, are not suitable for any living being and are merely the most cost-effective, simple, and accurate method of getting materials to a non-Terran location. As to the rate of loss of deliveries to the destination (if I may call them that), it is almost negligible—a mere 1 in 1,025. I, myself, have sent off 4,234 loads and have only lost 4 deliveries!

***

Now then, on to the all-important question: propulsion of live beings to the destination. As I have stated before, my balloon delivery system will not work as well for living beings, and so I have devised other means to convey myself to Mars. It, too, is a simple one and quite affordable. I had all my financial obligations of this project met (most obligingly) by one bank in one night.

The major cost of this method lies in the

shielding and safety features that all living beings require—as well as the life-support systems. The initial launch of a being into orbit is much the same as for my deliveries. The housing model for the live being (myself) in this example was built out of repurposed large rocket and airplane fuselage (as obtained from various airplane and rocket graveyards). The shape of this module is a tetrahedron, with six medium-sized protrusions and indentations on various faces, which are similar, in fact, to good old Lego blocks. These protrusions and indentations will be covered until orbit is achieved. More about that later.

***

Now, the module with the live being, or the bean module as I like to call it, contains the bare necessities for 72 hours of life-support—this for mass reasons. Other modules (up to 255, as a matter of fact, depending on your needs) will be deployed in the launch method of deliveries, but without Sunscreemers. These modules (I have used 63) will be of the utmost importance once the bean module achieves orbit. As to how the bean module is launched, nothing could be simpler.

The initial phase, as alluded to before, utilises

balloons once more. At the 20,000 foot mark, these balloons will be abandoned as the updraft from the supercell storm starts to draw the bean module higher into the troposphere. Here is where the deviations from the non-bean modules and the deliveries occur. The bean module does not use gunpowder for propulsion (that would be asking for trouble). Instead, an ingenious three-phase system of propulsion is utilised.

The first stage, whilst in the supercell storm, uses the differences in the outside atmospheric pressure and the propulsion unit, which is nothing more than compressed air. Once the atmospheric pressure is optimal, the bean module pierces the compressed air unit, thus propelling the bean module and its two other propulsion units higher into the atmosphere—much like a champagne bottle cork when you are a little bit too enthusiastic.

The phase two propulsion unit of the bean module would have, by this time, come into play. This unit is filled with water. Heat from friction will heat the water, and once the bean module has pierced this unit, the steam will propel the bean unit higher! I'm told this phase makes a sound reminiscent of old kettles, but I cannot verify that myself.

And finally, the third propulsion unit comes into play. This unit utilises blasts of air for propulsion and navigation, much like a leaf-blower. Point of fact, they are merely four modified leaf-blower systems affixed and shielded against the heat and such of these processes.

***

Now that the bean module has achieved orbit, the coverings are jettisoned and the protrusions and indentation are used to snap the non-bean modules to the bean module and thus build, through an automated sequence, a really big spaceship capable of sustaining a living human for a period of three years.

You will have surmised that the non-bean bearing modules will be carrying life-support materials as well as equipment for the human or humans on board. I do caution, however, that no more than 16 bean modules should be used per a spaceship, otherwise we have a logistics meltdown quite literally.

***

Each spaceship is fitted out with solar/magnetic drives, which work on solar flare principles. Thus, there is a short, but predictable period every 8 to 12 years, which is highly advantageous to this method of conveyance within our solar system. I speak, naturally, of solar storms. Timing is thus the most critical factor in the success of this method, especially if you (like me) wish to arrive at Mars within a year.

***

And there you have it; the most cost-effective and quick way to convey both materials and humans to any other rock in our solar system. I have already set up my base on Mars (with some amazingly new and accurate projectile systems), so I suggest you explore elsewhere in our large system.

May gravity cease to see your faults. I thank you.

This fictional article first appeared in Mad Scientist Journal in 2015, editors Dawn Vogel and Jeremy Zimmerman, illustrated by Shannon Legler.

FANTASY: LOCATION, SCOTLAND

Amusement

He would have been just as beautiful standing in a midden or a coalpit.

Beauty, in all its forms, was in his nature. As was deception.

But like its very nature—like his very nature—you didn't notice it until it was too late.

For me it had been far, far too late...and by then there was nothing to be done about it.

He stood in the circle, that bright October day, sunlight throwing glints onto his dark hair; his brilliant, clear grey eyes hidden behind classic sunglasses. He hadn't changed at all, not in ten years. Perhaps, he would never change, even in a thousand. And I finally understood. I finally saw what I had not these past ten roller-coaster years; ten years during which I had thought I had been saving him and he had been saving me; ten years during which we had been healing each other as it had been destined to be... But even destiny, it seems, has a glamour of its own.

He stood there, against the brilliant green hills, a thin stream sparkling like a line of energy behind him. He didn't need such a setting to highlight his beauty. He would have been just as beautiful standing in a midden or a coal-pit. Beauty, in all its forms, was in his nature. As was deception. But like its very nature—like *his* very nature—you didn't notice it until it was too late. For me it had been far, far too late...And by then there was nothing to be done about it.

I knelt down in the tall grass, half-hidden, camera at the ready. At this angle he seemed larger than life—a huge backlit shadow of some long-lost god of the place. I framed my picture to perfection. He seemed unaware, his gaze lost in the distance. I clicked the shutter button. He turned then, presenting me with his back, as always, like the ravens had at Aberdour. I sighed, wondering if I would ever get a decent picture of him. My legs were cramping. I stood up.

"It's a gorgeous day," he remarked in his offhand manner.

"Yes, it is," I agreed, my mind on his possible intentions of bringing me to this place again. He hadn't told me yet.

He put one boot on a stone to adjust his bootlaces. The impact of that boot made a dull thud that sent a small ripple through the valley like a tremor before the quake. I knew better than to be afraid. If he had wanted to hurt me, I would have been broken already...Wouldn't I? I began putting my camera away, fumbling it gracelessly as I tried to push it securely into the full daypack. He watched me indulgently. Ages later, I pulled the cord tight, snapped the fasteners securely then swung the bag onto my shoulders.

"Come here."

I hesitated, the invitation bringing back a rush

of memory and emotions. Another October, a lifetime ago, when he had stood in this same spot and I…I had feared that he would be stolen away by the *Sidhe,* like Tam Lin and Thomas the Rhymer —True Thomas who never once warned us we should beware the truth.

"Come here."

***

They had come, as I had half-feared and to my total disbelief. Things like that just did not happen in modern day Scotland, did they? But true-love kept you safe; and holding onto your true-love —no matter what—made the frustrated, defeated *Sidhe* leave you in peace. Or so they all say: all the ballads, all the folk-tales, all the wise ones. You just needed to hold on and be brave. *They cannae take wha's no theirs…*

So, I had held onto him that day as he had stood in that circle and I on the edge. I had held onto him tightly, clutching him to me, poring out my love for him—my truest love, my eternal love and adoration.

She had laughed mockingly, the fairy queen, in her jodhpurs and tightly pulled back silky ponytail. He had stood implacably, immovable, like warm breathing stone—calm and in control. I had shut my eyes tight against her piercing, mocking gaze.

"You'll come with me now," she commanded.

I had clutched at him tighter, hearing her compelling tone.

"Go to hell," he had told her equably.

Her amusement faded instantly. The day, warm and bright before, had suddenly seemed foreboding. He hugged me closer. I couldn't breath properly; his warm scent filling my nostrils—honeysuckle and fresh greenery. I half-turned my head so that I wouldn't suffocate, opening one eye to find her giving us a calculating look.

"Very well. Have it your way. You always do." Her gaze was on me again, pitiful, almost sympathetic. "Be careful what you wish for." She smiled humourlessly with pearly-white teeth any toothpaste ad agency would swoon to sport. She turned away, her silent host with her, to gallop off; leaving me with aching fingers and him with a creased shirt.

I hadn't known then what I knew now. I needn't have held onto him at all. He had his own protection against her.

***

"Come here." His voice, always soft and compelling, was more so than ever. He beckoned me with a long, gracefully-fingered hand.

I took a couple of faltering footsteps, stopping short of the circle. He smiled encouragement. That beautiful smile had always been my undoing. His hand guided me over the stones. He pulled me into his arms, binding—like honeysuckle or sticky willow. I didn't know what to expect: a ripple like the one his boot had made; a kaleidoscopic shifting into another dimension; or perhaps a burst of energy like a space-craft's tractor beam teleporting us into faery.

But he was not of the Sidhe.

He did not belong to them. He belonged only to himself.

And who did I belong to? It certainly wasn't to myself. Did I belong to him still, after the long year of heart-wrenching tearing away from him? I didn't know. Would I ever know?

I waited for that shifting of the world.

Nothing happened. The birds were still tweeting, the stream still sparkling, the grass still green. He chuckled. I had always been able to amuse him. Maybe that's what had won me his affection—his slightly mocking amusement at me—the graceless, elephant-footed incomer townie.

"That's what I love about you; always expecting the amazing when it's only ever going to be mundane." He was looking down at me, smiling, his face half in shadow.

I still couldn't see those eyes.

"I don't think meeting the fairy queen is mundane," I pointed out.

"No," he agreed. "But stepping into this circle is."

I still tried to read his expression. It was easier to sense what he was feeling, or rather what he wanted me to sense he was feeling. All I could get now was amused affection. I didn't trust it. I had learnt not to after I had felt his anger at me, in all its destructive force, not so very long ago.

I had thought he had wanted to kill me then. I had dreamt of him pursuing me, finding me where-ever had I tried to hide, until he had finally caught me and started to strangle me. A psychic attack, my aunt had informed me.

Can you really be murdered in your dreams? I had awoken, choking, before I could find out; trembling, terrified, knowing that I had lost a protection—his protection—without fully realising I had held it in the first place.

There was no anger now as he looked down at me, his finger gently tilting my face to his. Only that amused affection. He had always been slow to anger, building to a simmer, only to explode in volcanic fury when a line had been crossed. I had crossed that line when I had decided that enough was enough. I didn't want him back in my life ever again. I'd even stopped writing then, wanting a whole new life. But ever again can be an incredibly short time. I couldn't help but wonder if he was still simmering below my perception, getting ready to erupt at me as I had seen him do at others.

"Are you still afraid of me?" he asked, serious, his head cocked like a curious Labrador.

I slid my eyes away from those masking glasses, across his blue-green shirt and brown leather jacket to the comfortless green grass. Somewhere a cow lowed mournfully.

"Sometimes," I answered truthfully.

He knew anyway. I could never block my thoughts and feelings from him no matter how hard I tried or what methods I used. He reached through circles of light no matter their colour. He slipped through both angels and guardians. Protective crystals were regarded with frank amusement.

"You don't really want to block him. You leave the way open for him," my friend, the spiritual counsellor, had told me in exasperation. "You need to de-cord. Get back the power that you gave to him. Heal yourself."

That had been three years ago. The de-cording, then, had partially worked; he seemingly distracted by other things to pay much attention to what I was attempting. I had cried for a week, trying desperately not to miss him, trying to wean myself off him even though he was already over six thousand miles away from me.

"Hi. Are you okay?" he had asked me, and all my resolve had died.

All attempts at resisting him had flown through the window. I had missed him like I had missed a part of myself which I desperately needed to function.

"I'm fine. I love you." I had basked in his unseen presence, all my tears dried, all my misery and loneliness disappearing like wisps of mist in the sunlight.

"You should never be afraid of me. I'll always protect you."

And from yourself? I couldn't help but think.

His unseen eyes bore into me. "I would never hurt you, you know that."

"But you have! More than I thought anyone ever could." I didn't know how much I had voiced. It didn't matter. It never did. We had never really needed speech to communicate.

"I know. And I'm truly sorry. That had never been my intention."

"What was your intention?" I had to know.

It was the question which had been eating away at me ever since I had realised what he had done. How I had been deceived like the spider deceives the fly. How incredibly hopeless my fight had been. He had always called the tune—master musician that he was. And I had danced for him. Like his personal fool. Like his puppet, capering about in delight, never realising the cost. It wasn't just your feet that got sore.

His hand dropped but his gaze didn't faltered.

He hadn't answered the question. It wasn't the first time I had asked. It probably wouldn't be the last.

"Why have you brought me here?" I had to clear my throat. I didn't want to cry again, to show my weakness. He knew it well already, but I did have my pride.

He deigned to answer. "I wanted to show you something. I think you'll like it."

I tilted my head quizzically. "What?"

"Close your eyes," was all he said.

Slowly, I obeyed.

He tilted my chin again with those elegant, sensitive fingers and kissed my lips chastely.

I opened my eyes in surprise, my mind and vision starting to flood with memories and impressions formed ten years ago. I felt the delight and joy I had experienced when I had first visited Scotland. The burst of creativity raising me out of the ever-present depression. I could see again the vivid colours of the contrasting landscapes that had awed and fascinated me, as well as the people I had met with their humour and kindness to a gawky, strange foreigner.

I remembered seeing him for the first time—the love I had felt for him without even recognising it. The misery, too, at the thought that I had lost him along with the intense rush of joy of regaining him. I could feel again the contentment at the realisation that he would always be with me, and me with him, no matter where in the world I happened to be. I needed no picture of him because he was in my heart. He broke off the kiss, leaning back to look down at me, smiling.

"Do you know now?" he asked, smugly.

I nodded. I knew. I loved him. I hated him. My relationship with him would always be tumultuous. He was my saviour, my detractor, my best friend, my worst enemy. He was the villain of my life, the hero I could not live without....

"You're my muse," I whispered the revelation in wonder.

He nodded once, smiling in pleasure—a teacher at a star pupil. "Now you've got it." He kissed my forehead. "Hot chocolate?" he suggested.

"Good idea," I hugged him affectionately, stepping out of the circle. The drum of hooves brought me up short.

His arm went protectively around me.

"You're back." observed the fairy queen with that more than toothpasty smile.

"You'll never have her. She's mine." His voice was cold.

She stared at us. "Pity. I could have done so much with her."

I stared at them in incomprehension.

She laughed suddenly at his stern countenance. "Fair's fair, I suppose. But I'll have the next one." She sped off down the field laughing. I shivered.

He took off his jacket, draping it around my shoulders. "There's a hot chocolate with your name on it," he reminded me, pulling me towards the waiting car.

I resisted a moment, taking in the empty field, its circle and the vivid colours. Then I followed him—half in joy, half in fear. Like I always do.

This story, written in 2010 and inspired by my favourite Diana Wynne Jones story, first appeared in SeeThroughIt Mag Special Mini Edition.

FANTASY: LOCATION, THE KALAHARI DESERT, SOUTH AFRICA

Martinus Meerkat Man

Perfectly framed. Martinus was in professional heaven in that detached way cameramen have when behind the lens.
Snick. The Gemsbok looked up startled.
Snick. It turned tail.
Snick. Snick...

The Kalahari sands lay red, hinting at the dangers they hid—Red Romans, Rhinkhals and perhaps an outraged meerkat or two. Speaking of which, Martinus Meerkat Man was on a dune hidden by a convenient shrub, watching the gemsbok through his sights, waiting for that perfect shot. It wouldn't be long now, he knew.

Beside him, his pet meerkat, Morden, perked up from his scorpion snack, sniffing, swinging his head this way and that like an old radar dish on unoiled pivots. Then he scurried to the top of Martinus' head to stare at the storm-clouded horizon.

Below Morden, Martinus had found his perfect shot.

Double-checking that he was on multi-shot, he pressed the shutter button. It was the start, in every sense, of the perfect series of stills.

Perfectly framed, Martinus was in professional heaven in that detached way cameramen have when behind the lens.

Snick.

The gemsbok looked up startled.

Snick.

It turned tail.

Snick. Snick.

The buck began to run, its long legs seeming to grow longer, presenting differing views of its magnificent horns.

Snick. Snick.

It was galloping now.

Morden went crazy, scurrying atop Martinus' head, almost sliding off, half-blinding him. But Martinus got Morden's foot off his sunglasses in time to see the most perfect shoot ever.

The rush of air wasn't enough to prepare the photographer who had seen everything.

Snick. Snick. Snick.

The tail seemed almost to touch the chittering Morden.

Martinus didn't have time to look up from the viewfinder as the dragon brushed by like a CZ at the air-show, complete with a gust of warmed air of what might have been afterburners but was probably dragon-breath.

Snick. Snick. Snick.

The dragon, in its whole serpentine length, was caught in all its glory.

Snick. Snick. Snick.

The gemsbok, at full gallop, with the dragon gaining.

Snick. Snick. Snick. Crunch.

The dragon's catching of the poor, stunned bok by its gems carried clearly through the silence; to be broken almost immediately by the sonic boom of the dragon shooting straight up into the atmosphere, disappearing faster than that CZ at 25,000 feet at the air-show.

Martinus grinned hugely.

Perfect!

###

One of my first attempts at flash-fiction, this story first appeared in See ThroughIt Mag Special Mini Edition.

BONUS STORY

a WA Short Story
WALPOLE WERE
He'll roo
the day...
leenna naidoo

He stood by the tree, barely discernible in the dusk shadows. The family of kangaroos grazing on the lawn before the forest of Tinglewoods ignored him. He posed no threat, their instincts informed them, and rightly so. He was no hunter of kangaroos or other fauna. No, his entire focus was on his oblivious subject—the Lesser-Spotted-Single-Female-Holidaymaker; sitting on the deck of the cottage with a glass of wine, a big packet of Grainwaves, and her camera.

The wind suddenly picked up, blowing over the scent of the backburning fifteen kilometres away. The kangaroos jerked up, noses twitching, scanning the area. He stood stock-still, not wanting to startle the animals. When they left she would go inside, he knew, watching as she quickly and expertly shot off some photos. The sun backlit the trees as it neared setting. Above him, leaves fluttered on the wind's breath. Somewhere, high above and to the right, a kookaburra laughed. He sighed as he watched its ghostly shape glide up to the deck bannister. It ruffled its feathers, seemingly bringing itself into focus, then turned to look expectantly at her and her camera.

"I'm not going to feed you. I was told not to—

you greedy little thing." Her voice, a little subdued but affectionate, carried clearly in the sudden lull.

'Good on yer,' he thought.

***

He had noticed her Kia drive up to the cottage just as he was packing away the final samples for the day, eager to investigate the strange spoor which had distracted him earlier in the afternoon. Once his official tasks were done, he followed the trail. To his surprise, it had led back here. One lonely imprint lay faintly near the barbed-wire fence separating the forest from the lawn of the four holiday cottages. The mark next to him was deeper than any of the others. The animal, like him, had stood there under the tree.

The strange paw-like spoor was immediately forgotten once he looked up directly into her camera. He stiffened in outrage, then realised she probably couldn't see him, with the lowering sun throwing the shade of the trees into inky blackness. Noticing the kangaroos, he relaxed. They were part of the reason Frank's cottages were usually with a renter or two. There were *always* kangaroos on the spacious lawns, as advertised.

Frank had mentioned, the previous day, that

a strange woman had booked the smallest cottage for a week. "....all by herself. That's a lot of space for one, but there's no families till the holidays, so..."

Frank and Ella would have given her a tour of the cottage and facilities, then left. The furthest cottage was also in use, with the two middle ones empty. Not bad for the off-peak. Most businesses were hurting with the rise of the dollar and the cutbacks in public transportation in this part of the South West—the whole of the West, to be honest.

He sighed again. At least the trees would always be here—as long as he took good care of them.

The wind was growing cooler. The Lesser-Spotted-Single-Female-Holidaymaker shivered, shut off her camera then carried her wine and chips inside. She carefully shut the screen-door before pulling the sliding door close. The curtains were drawn next. He stood there a few seconds longer, entranced.

The light had faded to twilight blue quite fast. His sharp eyes had only just been able to make out the strong features framed by the frizz of hair. Her expression had been hard to place. It took him a second to identify it: silent joy. He grinned, hefted his pack and headed off to his ute, all the while wondering how to approach such an elusive creature. Instinct told him that, while she was fine taking photos of roos and talking to kookaburras, she might be skittish of *Homo Sapiens*. He would go suss out things with Frank and Ella. They always appreciated knowing how the forest was doing.

***

Augustine, Gusty to his friends, rose cautiously from the forest floor. He'd followed the unsuspecting forester along his own track from the previous night. He smiled grimly as the man, gawking at the woman in the cottage, never knew how close he'd been to death with his neck and back so exposed. He didn't bother following the forester back. It was a small community. It would be easy enough to find the man. Gusty flexed his hands. With an anticipatory gaze, he walked over to the spot where the forester had been standing.

He'd have to pay the lady a special visit. He was glad she'd been given the cottage he'd hidden the *TeaPot* in. It made retrieving it all that much sweeter, killing two birds with one stone. Her blood would do well for his spell.

I downloaded the pics of the kangaroos and kookaburras with satisfaction. It was a joy to see them behaving so naturally this close to humans. The male had been a little scary, taller than me when he had picked up his head and stood straight—a little over the six-feet I'd been told to expect.

The kookaburra, too, had proved an interesting subject; puffing and preening, looking directly at the camera with a regal expression. I'd known then this trip was going to be special. Spotting obliging wildlife, even if they weren't my focus, was an excellent portent. And *They,* my little telepathic grapevine of Grandma's kin, had been chatty ever since I'd entered this part of the South West. Hardly surprising with the gorgeous old forest on both sides of the roads I'd driven. It was exciting to see Grandma (who'd been a *dryad,* and sadly no cryptoid) had been right about her Australian cousins—the Tinglewoods; a gregarious and affectionate bunch as trees go. I'd felt the affection, but only gotten snatches of the conversations and greetings. I guess I drive at faster than tree-thoughts. And here, from the forest just beyond the cabin, *They*'d sent me waves of fragrant welcome. I would go visit them tomorrow.

I logged into my website next. No new sightings had been made since I'd last checked twenty-four hours ago. I took a few moments to click through my new photos. The kangaroos looked quite adorable. My niece would be ecstatic. I frowned at the one with the joey in mid-scratch. There, far in the background almost indiscernible in the shadow of the big tree, was the man who'd been watching me. It had creeped me out at first. I'd decided to ignore him; he seemed harmless enough. Besides *They* had told me he meant no harm and that his name was Ash—a good strong arboreal name. That meant *They* liked him—probably a lot.

I stared at the photo, zoomed in as far as I could without the pixels mushing into incoherence. Ash was tall, what I thought of as rangy. His hair looked unkempt like a Manga character's. His feet were slightly apart, one knee bent, his whole silhouette conveying alertness like the male kangaroo when I'd first stepped out with my wine and chips. I shook my head with a rueful smile—curious natives, that's all—then went on to what was really important: working on the introduction to my new paper on Australian Cryptozoology. I had a feeling it was going to be a good one.

***

"Said her name's Stacy. No, she didn't say what she does," said Frank. "Struck me as a geologist, or something. We've had a few going through here recently, now the mines are back on track. We're not that far from the mining belt, you know, for a weekend away. Another glass?"

Ash shook his head. "No, thanks. Early start tomorrow. There's still the soil samples to take. We're a mite concerned about the new dieback outbreak in SA. We don't think it will reach us, but the rainy season still has a way to go."

"And you never know who's been walking in the woods these days," added Ella, bringing two wrapped parcels to the coffee-table as Ash stood up. "Here. Fresh out the oven. One's for you and the other's for Stacy, if you wouldn't mind dropping it off for me," she said, twinkling at the look of amusement in his hazel eyes. "I'd say you and her have a lot in common judging by the way her eyes lit up when she first saw the forest outside the cottage."

"Thanks, Ella." Ash accepted the parcels. "I'll stop by the cottage first chance I get. Stacy, was it?"

"Yes," smiled back Frank with a wink. "Walk you to the road."

"Bye, Ella," called Ash, preceding Frank through the door.

Both men walked side by side down to the gate.

"You think those tracks were foxes?" asked Frank.

"No, definitely not. Too big."

"Dingo?"

"Nope. Don't know what they are yet. Definitely not local wildlife or ferals. Already notified both the Wildlife and Parks, and Customs. It's likely someone's smuggled in some kind of exotic dog...or wolf."

Frank looked worried. He had grown up on a farm, but had always preferred relocating roos to shooting them. He was fond of all the local wildlife and didn't like the idea of another imported predator out there. "You gonna try and catch it?"

"Yeah. Some boys from Perth Zoo are driving down to come help. They arrive tomorrow with a cage."

"Good, good." Frank patted Ash on his arm. "If you need any help—"

"I know how to reach you," laughed Ash. "Goodnight, Frank."

"Night, Ash." He watched Ash lope off into the night. Frank shook his head. That apple hadn't fallen far from the tree.

***

Gusty stood under the tree watching the cottages. No lights were on in either of the rentals. Even the little critters were silent knowing something big and powerful was about. He smiled knowing it was him they sensed and feared. Nothing in the world was going to strip this power away from him, not once he got his hand on the *TeaPot*.

A quarter moon had risen late in the chilled sky. He glanced at his phone, 2:30a.m, before slipping it back into his pocket. It was time to pay the lady a visit.

***

I awoke suddenly, wondering what had disturbed me. I could just about hear the wind in the trees outside, and *They* were silent. The wooden cottage creaked a little here and there. No other alarming sounds. I rolled over, reaching an arm out for my phone—2:30a.m—too early for kangaroos or exploring. I snuggled back under the covers.

***

Gusty crept up onto the wooden deck. Not a board creaked. Reaching the screen sliding door, he finessed it open. The glass door followed, sliding half open with barely a whisper. Carefully, he secured the screen door halfway, preventing it rolling back with a bang, and offering him a quick getaway.

Gusty snuck inside and stood against the glass door. He was in the living room leading to the dining area. He wouldn't bother with the kitchen to the left of the dining-room. The opposite sliding door led to the back deck with another smaller wooden door leading off the deck and into the laundry and bathroom. Gusty dropped down onto all fours and stretched his back. It lengthened, as did his nose. Thirty seconds later Gusty was a tall, grey mangy wolf—a fairy-tale cliché.

He boldly padded into the main bedroom, following her scent—tea tree and ginger—a vaguely familiar smell... Half a second was all it took to see she wasn't in the bed, still undisturbed from its pristine presentation to guests. On the bag-stand lay a big blue gear-bag. He sniffed it curiously. Why would she leave such a big gear-bag in the main bedroom? He didn't have time for strange tourist quirks. His bloodlust was growing. And so was his need for the *TeaPot* with the client losing patience, and the spell needing to be done before he handed it over.

She had to be in the other bedroom.

***

My eyes flew open, all sleepiness vanishing. *They* were warning me. Someone, or something, was in the house. I rolled over, grabbing for my pepper-spray and camera as I slipped into my boots. That's when I had my confirmation. I grinned. The system worked.

***

Gusty stepped into the living-room, moving purposefully towards the second bedroom. A mechanical whirring was the first indication that things might be headed in an unexpected direction. He pricked his ears, muzzle retreating to reveal cruel fangs.

The first flash hit him in the eye, startling him.

He cringed back, whining in surprise, his paws clicking on the wooden floor. A quick succession of flashes followed, coming from every direction, encircling him. Just when they stopped, a huge violet flash blasted him away. Trembling, Gusty regained his paws shakily. What the—? Then the lady was bearing down on him, camera in one hand, pepper spray in the other.

Gusty didn't stop to think. He turned tail and ran for the door. *Her hand was pulling his tail!* With tremendous effort, Gusty dived for the gap in the doorway, skidded through with a yelp and bounded off into the night. Behind him, he heard her crash into the glass door. He raced for the safety of the forest. What the *hell* was all that about? And why had that last violet flash made him feel so...*violated?* Gusty tried to run faster, but failed.

***

My shoulder hurt from when I'd bounced off the glass-door. Fortunately, it was shatterproof or something and looked none the worse for wear. I panted, elated, watching the faint lupine form disappear into the dark of the forest.

That wolf wasn't natural. This was it: my

first ever meeting with a Were. My hand! It was covered with his fur—a sample; viable I hoped. I looked at the Violet Light camera. Its red blinking LED meant it was charging. A good night, or rather morning, then. Delighted, I hurried to the kitchen in search of a sample bag for the fur.

***

The ute's clock read 8:30a.m. It still seemed a little too early for social calls even though Ash could see her, sitting out on the back deck, as he drove up. He had planned on looking for more of those unusual tracks, but seeing this Stacy first meant he wouldn't be thinking about her all day.

He pulled up next to her Kia, took a deep breath, and, not daring to look at her, turned off the engine. She had stood up by then. He stepped out of the ute cradling Ella's parcel and called out, "Hi! I'm Ash. Ella asked me to drop this off for you."

"Oh!" Her eyebrows had shot up. "I didn't think...She didn't have to."

"It's her incredibly famous shortbread," grinned Ash.

"Well, in that case, please come in. I'm Stacy, by the way."

She smiled at him. He smiled back. A few moments slid by as their eyes met, her green to his tawny brown. Ash felt a strange thrill, like a thunderstorm approaching. It had to be her because he knew the sky above was its customary cerulean with nary a hint of a cloud, even a faint wispy one.

She cleared her throat. "I'll just go put the kettle on."

She dove into the cottage. Ash shut the ute door before following her in, half bemused, half thrilled.

***

"Tea or coffee?" she asked as he placed the parcel on the dining-room table.

"Coffee, please."

"Decaff okay?"

"Decaff's fine," replied Ash, sitting down at the table as a kookaburra landed on the deck-rail outside, eyeing the abandoned plate which had held Stacy's toast.

"So are you staying here for a day or two?" he asked, watching as she readied two mugs, sugar, milk, and some teaspoons.

"Oh no. The whole week! I was originally planning on only staying here for three nights, then four in Denmark, but it's so beautiful here that I decided a week would be better."

"You've made the right choice, especially if you just want to relax." Ash's eyes roamed over the living room and the half-opened bedroom door. He frowned slightly, taking in the rumpled sheets in what he knew wasn't the main bedroom. Then there were all those cameras positioned in the living room. "What is it that you do, Stacy?"

"I'm a researcher and writer."

"Is that why all the cameras?"

"Yep."

The water boiled. Ash waited till she had poured the water in the two mugs before remarking, "I haven't seen your friend, or is it partner?"

Stacy glanced at him sharply as she set down a steaming mug in front of him along with the sugar and a teaspoon. "My friend?"

He gestured towards the bedroom. "I thought..."

"Oh!" laughed Stacy, going back to the kitchen. "I was watching the kookaburra and fell asleep."

"Oh, right. Done that a few times myself," laughed Ash, a little confused.

Stacy sat down at the table, placed milk near him and picked up a teaspoon. "And what do you do when you're not delivering neighbourhood parcels?"

"I'm a forester. Patrol most of this area of the Nornalup and halfway to Pemberton."

"Really?" exclaimed Stacy, perking up so much that Ash wondered if she going to make fun of him. "Tell me, and I know this is going to sound weird, but have you noticed any strange, any...alien, animals around here?"

He stared at her suspiciously.

"No, seriously. I'd really like to know. And I'd keep it completely confidential. I'm a cryptozoologist, you see."

"A crypto...You study strange, mythical, unscientific animals?" Ash was sure she was taking the mickey.

"Yep. And there's nothing unscientific about it. Take for instance, the coelacanth. Who would have believed it if the fisherman hadn't brought in samples—proof!"

Ash could see she was filing him away with all the others she'd had to justify herself to. He didn't want that. He wanted her—needed her—to trust him, to be herself with him.

His mother had always told him he'd *just know*

when he found the right woman for him and, dammit, she was right again. Stacy…,whatever her surname was, was going to be his woman. He knew it in his bones, in his heart. He couldn't make fun of something so important to her so he said, "As a matter of fact, I *have* seen some strange spoor. Think it might be some kind of canine."

Her eyes sparkled with excitement, but she didn't say anything, just looked at him like he was her hero.

"I was just going to check them out again after I'd dropped off the parcel." On impulse, he added, "Wanna come? I could have you back here in…three, maybe four, hours."

***

I could have kissed him then, this beautiful man with his warm tawny eyes in that long friendly face, but I didn't. Being so impulsive had gotten me into trouble too many times before. I was now much more mature and proud of it.

"Just give me three minutes!" I told him, abandoning my coffee to rush into the bedroom, only just remembering to shut the door.

I shucked off my sleeping shorts, dragged on my jeans, slipped into my boots and tied up my laces. My T-shirt was next, a swap for a clean one, before grabbing my always set-to-go backpack. I ran my fingers briefly through my hair, swept up my hair band and stepped into the dining room.

Ash looked at me in surprise. "Wow! You weren't kidding. I think you can finish you coffee, though. It's barely gotten cold," he said with admiration.

It was then, I think, that I fell in love with him.

***

The forest was cool, abuzz with insects. I followed in Ash's footsteps, annoyed with myself for admiring his long back and broad shoulders instead of taking note of my surroundings or chatting to my distant kin. Even *They* seemed amused, not giving me any further information like they usually would. "So when was it you first noticed this odd spoor?" I asked.

"About a week ago, maybe. The animal's been here much longer. The rains came late and the ground was too hard to hold a good print before."

"Less than a year, then?" I prompted, wanting to hear more of his quiet, thoughtful voice.

"Yeah, definitely less than eight months. More likely four at most, I'd say. If it stayed the winter, it should be shedding now. Might be able to get a fur sample."

My heart thumped with my half desperation to tell him about my early-morning visitor, but would he believe me? I'd been lucky, so far, that Ash seemed to like me and had not run off freaked out like most guys. And I really didn't want him to. I thought—hoped—Ash would be different. So, I held my tongue as I followed him carefully through the beautiful, friendly but quiet, aromatic forest.

***

Gusty, attempting sternness, stared at his reflection in the mirror. He'd taken ages to quit trembling. Afterwards, he'd still had to retrieve his clothes. It had been almost dawn by then. Luckily, no one had seen him. Just looking at that cabin again had given him the chills. The *TeaPot* was still in there...

And time was running out.

He had to get it back. The client was flying into Margaret River in two days. There was no way to buy more time, not with with him needing to do the spell before handing it over. Why had he put it off for so long? The thought of losing his Were powers after the next full moon filled him with terror almost as great as the one the client had instilled in him.

What had happened to him at the cabin? What had all those cameras been doing in that place? Did they catch his change? He didn't think so, but he couldn't take a chance. He had to go back, had to get those cameras, and make sure they hadn't captured him. More importantly, he had to get the *TeaPot* this time. If he didn't…

Gusty shivered again imagining the consequences.

***

With Ash stopping every now and then to take notes, we found a newer spoor not an hour or so into the forest.

The spoor meandered back parallel to the way we'd come, presumably ending somewhere near my cabin. We followed the faint track in the opposite direction, briefly lost it on the main Denmark route, then regained it across the road. A few metres into the forest, Ash stopped, stooping down for a closer look. I crowded in, camera ready. His long fingers hovered over the strange prints. I shut my mouth and snapped away.

The first print looked like a messy paw-print, or a mangled one. The next showed the suggestion of five toes and the curve of a humanoid foot. The third looked wholly human.

"It must be your lucky day, Stacy, or some-one's playing the joker," remarked Ash, unfazed, his calm brown eyes on me.

"Let's hope I'm lucky then," I said unthinking, then blushed.

Amusement, after a brief spark in his eye. He stood up with a smile, leading the way again. The spoor ended at the Bibbulman Track. Ash uttered an all-purpose Aussie adjectival verb while I just thought, *dammit!*

***

Gusty lurked at the edge of the forest, eyeing the two in the cabin. They'd arrived almost an hour into his surveillance, just when he'd decided to make his move. A simple break-in, that's all. Just five lousy minutes; and he couldn't even get that! He'd never had such a run of bad luck before. He was usually other people's bad luck.

The forester guy, Ash Andersson, was stick-ing around. But he could deal with that lanky weakling easily. The woman too, as long as those cameras didn't go off. Gusty watched intently as they both ate a light lunch. His stomach growled, but he ignored it. He was on a mission, one he couldn't fail.

***

Ash smiled bashfully at Stacy, having flapped a serviette at her; one she had waved away, using her own to dab ineffectually at the spreading coffee stain on her clothes.

"Sorry I'm such a clumsy klutz," he said.

"Oh, it's okay. I do the same all the time. Just a minute, I'll go change."

She smiled back at him, making his heart jerk alarmingly.

She disappeared into the bedroom. Ash sighed in satisfaction. Lunch had been good: salmon wraps, good coffee, and some of Ella's biscuits. He looked around the living room again. Five cameras covered the area. Two lay on either end of the long bookshelf, while on the opposite side of the room, one stood on a sturdy tripod and the other perched on a sofa arm. The one on the chimney pipe and three others looked like standard point-and-shoot cameras. The fifth—the biggest one—was another matter. It stood on the bookshelf looking large and unwieldy, like it had been cobbled together from other cameras. Its large old-fashioned round flashbulb stared at the room. Ash frowned.

Stacy found him crouched, examining the VL-Cam intently.

"Interesting camera," he remarked.

"Yes. It was built especially for me."

Ash waited but she didn't elaborate. "Why do you need so many cameras?"

"A cryptozoologist always needs proof."

"Do you have to be so cryptic?" She didn't smile or laugh, just stared back at him.

***

I knew then that I had to tell Ash. The changing footprints hadn't freaked him out. He had taken it in his stride remarkably well. Maybe—*hopefully*—he was one of those rare people who accepted what their eyes saw as much as their hearts did. He was looking at me all expectant. I opened my mouth, wondering how to explain, then held up a finger. "Just a moment, please." It would be easier to show him.

"It's kinda hard to explain," I began, carrying my laptop over to the living-room. "Violet light has remarkable properties. Bear with me here. I know it sounds off topic, but do you know of those cameras which scan your aura?"

He had that bemused look again. "Your funny camera takes aura photos?"

"Not exactly. It's best if you see…Why does this thing take so long to launch? Sorry. I keep meaning to upgrade, but… Anyway, last night, early this morning, I had a…visitor."

"A visitor?" He'd gotten up to come stand next to me as I set the laptop down on the table.

"Yes, a…a Werewolf."

"A Were? Wolf?"

I nodded. Out of the corner of my eye, I saw a figure approaching. Vaguely, I wondered who it might be. My full attention was on choosing my next words with care. "I think that was what made the tracks. A Werewolf, not native, of course. It would have to have been an…immigrant."

"A Werewolf?" he said again, emphasising the 'wolf'.

"Yes." He stared back at me, his face blank, his eyes wary. I was losing him. "I have some evidence. The violet light—" Then, *They* were whispering for attention. The figure out on the lawn had disappeared. *They* were warning me. The Were!

"He's here!" I whispered, running for my room. Where had I left the pepper-spray and colloidal silver? On the dresser?

"Stacy, that's the craziest thing—," called Ash from the dining room. Then, "Oh, hi. Can I help you?"

Time was out. Frantically, I upended my backpack. My pepper spray rolled off the bed, and there was the small bottle of colloidal silver. I had to save Ash.

The Were spoke. "Where is she?"

"That's some strange hand you've got there," remarked Ash in a conversational way. "Are you part of that TV crew up the road?"

"Where is she?" roared the Were as I whipped around the corner, hitting the manual trigger for the VL-Cam with my knuckles, both bottle and spray at the ready.

Ash was already moving in a lazy fashion as the familiar flash of the VL-Cam went off. The Were hit the floor with a crash, shaking the cameras and dishes on the table. He rolled on the floor, alternately holding his stomach and his face.

"He attacked me. Had to kick him," explained Ash in his bland way, looking pale.

We stared at the Were rolling on the floor, narrowly avoiding the fallen coffee table. He now held one hand to his face and one to his stomach, obviously in terrible pain.

"We should call the police," suggested Ash faintly.

"And the Parks and Wildlife."

He looked at me in surprise. "Actually—" He fell over.

The Were had kicked the table towards us, hitting Ash's legs. I tripped over him in my efforts to chase the escaping Were, but he caught my ankle.

"Don't be stupid, Stacy." His voice was quiet, one eye hidden by his hair, the other bright and compelling.

A knock at the door broke the spell.

***

"Sorry to bother you folks," said a big guy at the back-door, "but is there an Ash Andersson here?"

He was trying not to look too enquiringly at the scene. Another thin guy in uniform joined him.

Ash, still sprawled on the floor, still holding my ankle, raised his hand. "I'm Ash. You must be the boys from Perth Zoo."

"That we are," confirmed the bear of a man.

Ash released me and stood up. "You just missed it."

"So we see," was the non-committal reply.

"You'd best sit down. Stacy here has something to show us."

"Ash, I don't think...," I began, bewildered and pretty sure the animal handlers wouldn't believe me. They were still standing just outside the door waiting patiently.

"It's okay, Stacy. These boys need to know what we're up against."

The bear man quirked an eyebrow. "Indeed we do. So you've identified the feral?"

"Right in this living-room."

The sharp-faced man looked keen. "Canid?"

Ash looked at me again, then back to the animal handlers. "You boys been up North?"

"Oh, yeah." and "Every year." They both looked askance.

Ash seemed to relax. "Stacy has something to show us," he repeated.

I looked at each man, then shrugged. "Alright, but you've got to keep an open mind," I warned.

"If I kept it open any wider, it would fall out, ma'am," reassured the bearlike guy matter-offactly. "I'm Chris and this is my mate, Steve. A Frank said for us to come over."

"That's okay. Please have a seat. I'll just open the files," I said with as much grace as I could muster.

Fortunately, the application opened quickly and up popped the photos of the Were's early-morning visit.

"There he is." I turned the screen towards my guests.

The men leaned in.

"It's a wolf, alright. Looks like a North American Grey," remarked Steve.

"Yep," agreed Chris.

"Bigger than your usual wolf," added Ash.

"Buggers been known to grow even bigger, but he's a fair-sized one. What's got you all het up about him, then?" asked Chris.

Ash looked at me as if to say *over to you*, so I said, "See that camera over there?" Chris and Steve looked at it obligingly. "It's a specially fitted one. It uses violet light, not quite UV, but safer and quite close to that spectrum. You may have heard of an Excimer Lamp?" They hadn't. "Well, this is kind of like it... Thing is, it's excellent in showing potential, as well as current states of a living being." They looked blankly back at me. "Well, it's like...Oh, never mind! Just look at this photo."

The blueish-purplish photo of the wolf filled the screen. Around the backtracking wolf was the glow of a human male, distinct enough to recognise his features right down to the cleft on his square jaw.

"Looks like Photoshop artsy stuff to me," stated Steve in a way I was now used to.

"I could download the original from my camera for you right now," I offered without missing a beat.

Chris, his deepening frown displaying his uneasiness, said, "No, no. I believe you. Seen some strange things in my life. Especially up North... at night." He was looking meaningfully at Ash who stared back equably. Then to me again, "So he's what fantasy writers call a shape-shifter, right?"

"No, he's what people call a Werewolf. They've been documented for the past five hundred years, at least. Sabine actually—"

"Yes, I've read Sabine," interrupted Chris. Then, "A real Werewolf...in our fair state." He shook his head slowly, sadly.

I almost felt sorry for the Werewolf.

***

"Wonder why he keeps coming back here? I mean, to this cabin," Steve remarked, staring thoughtfully into his cup of tea resting near the three tranquilliser rifles.

I'd convinced the three men to have some tea before heading off after the Werewolf, whose likeness had already been emailed to the local police along with an '*Approach with caution. Recommend tranquillise suspect*' advisory. The men looked at me; easy prey was what they were no doubt thinking. Perhaps they were right.

I turned to Ash. "What did he say to you?"

"He kept asking where you were," Ash answered. "Maybe he knows you?"

I shook my head. "I doubt it. Do you think he'll come back?"

"Dunno. If there was a specific reason," suggested Chris.

Steve followed with, "Maybe this was his cabin and he's being territorial. He attacked Ash, after all."

Ash nodded. "I'd better call Frank."

But Frank could not remember any renter who fitted the description. And then it was time to go into the forest. I carefully strung the VL-Cam around my neck while the guys picked up their gear. It had only one charge left, but it would have to do.

"Do you really have to take that thing?" asked Chris. "You know you shouldn't even be coming with us."

I stared him down. He looked meaningfully at Ash, who just shrugged and smiled at me. I smiled back. It seemed like ages since I had last seen that smile. I followed the guys out, locking the cabin behind me.

***

Gusty snarled, racing his Ford towards Denmark, the graze from the bullet smarting. Two cops had stopped him. Routine check, they'd said, but Gusty knew otherwise. Pity the one had been so quick, and that he hadn't the time to finish them off. He'd have to run for it now. That was okay. He still had to get that damned *TeaPot*, though. And with them hounding him down towards Denmark, the last thing they'd expect was him to backtrack to that cabin and then to Margaret River, using the forest as cover. Gusty's snarl morphed into a cold, evil smile. Payback time.

***

Ash was nervous walking behind Chris and Steve with Stacy beside him, though he hid it well. He wished Stacy had gone over to Frank and Ella's —some place safe; but he knew it would be useless to ask. She had the look of someone always in the midst of things, never on the sidelines. Besides, she'd earned it. She'd been right about the Were. Ash kept pace with Stacy, determined to protect her. Chris and Steve could handle the Were.

Now that he had time to think about it, Ash was frightened. A bloody Werewolf! Here in his back-yard! He could have been killed, Ash knew, re-membering the look in the guy's eye when he had sprung at him. The Were had been going straight for his jugular! Lucky for him, Ash grinned, he'd always had long legs and a good instinct.

"Here's about right." Chris scratched his head. From the edge of the trees to the left of Stacy's cabin, they could observe all the cabins and ap-proaches easily. "Steve, you wanna shimmy up that tree there and get a better look?"

Steve slung his rifle over his shoulders and took out slim rope from his backpack. He tossed the rope over some tree branches and used it climb up the first five metres or so of the smooth bole. He quickly disappeared into the canopy. Ash remained alert, scanning the area, ears twitching at every sound. Stacy joined Chris in surveying the cabins.

"Might take a few hours before he shows, if he shows," murmured Chris. "Steve, you alright up there?"

"Right as rain."

Ash sighed. It looked like it was going to be a long wait.

***

Gusty pulled up to the cabin. Only the girl's Kia was there. The boyfriend's truck was gone. Gusty snarled at the thought of him. The forester had kicked him right in the stomach! It still ached. When all this was over he'd settle that score, but for now, the *TeaPot* was first priority. Time for stealth over, Gusty went swiftly to the sliding door. It was locked.

"No worries, as they say." He turned to the left.

His grin was savage as he kicked in the laundry

door. Boldly, he walked in. Finally, the *TeaPot* was going to be his—replenishing his Were-power for another fifty years—before the client could get his paws on it.

***

Things happened so fast, I'm still not sure how it all went. I watched, along with the men, with bated breath as the Were first tried the sliding door of my cabin. Then, without a second's hesitation, he went directly to the laundry room door and kicked it violently open. He disappeared inside my cabin. I stared in shock, suddenly realising the danger I'd been in before. Beside me, I knew without looking that Ash had tensed, his fingers tightening on the rifle. Steve was already swinging down the tree, branches raining aromatic leaves down on us below.

"Okay, I'm going in. Steve, Ash, follow me." Then Chris was running down the slight incline to the cabin, rifle at the ready.

There were no windows on that side of the cabin, so any chance of the Were spotting us was small. Steve dropped down heavily, sprang up at once, and followed his partner.

Ash hesitated a second. "Stay here," he whispered, then ran after Steve, the rifle awkward in his grasp.

I focussed the camera on the scene and realised any photo I took would be fuzzy. Nothing for it but to get closer. I hurried behind Ash.

The Were appeared, with Chris just a couple of metres short of the wooden decking. Chris didn't falter. He meant to tackle the Were! Steve had immediately dropped down to one knee, balancing as he aimed his rifle. Ash veered left, out of Steve's way, moving towards the Were's black Ford. I stopped, dithering. Cover Chris or cover Ash, which would be the best shot? Erring on the side of caution, I followed Ash to cover both angles from the left.

I glanced up at a vicious snarl and a roar. Chris's tackle had missed, leaving him sprawled on the decking. The Were sprang over the rail and onto the bonnet of his car. Something whizzed nearby, hitting the car with a metallic twang—Steve's tranquilliser dart. Ash's momentum was as great as Chris's had been. He wouldn't have time to stop and shoot. He was almost to the car! The

Were had pulled open the driver's door, a small parcel in his hand. He threw it into the car and turned in a crouch to meet Ash's rush.

Finger on my VL-Cam at the ready, I stood horrified. The Were would tear Ash apart! Chris was up and moving, but he would be too late.

I expected Ash to swing the rifle, to at least club at the Were. Instead, in what looked like some kind of travesty of a running Irish Jig or a performance of *The Riverdance*, Ash once more fairly and squarely kicked the Were in the tummy.

The Were bounced off his car, into Ash's bent knee, bounced off his car again, headbutted Ash in the sternum, and crashed to the ground beneath a growling Chris. Chris's hand flashed with a metallic glint. I jerked in shock, triggering my VL-Cam. Half a second later, Chris had jabbed the tranquilliser into the squirming Were. I rushed to Ash's side. He was wheezing.

"You okay?" I set my camera on the grass. I'd need both hands to help Ash stand.

Chris stood up too, panting and weaving a little, moving back from the unconscious Were. Ash allowed me to help him stagger up. That's when Chris bumped into both of us.

We staggered about again like actors in a silent comedy.

A crunch, and Chris was saying, "Oops! Didn't see that there." He looked me in the eye with his sincere brown ones. "I'll get you another one," he promised.

I stared down at the smashed VL-Cam. Chris was a big man. He had all but stomped on it.

"It's okay," I said faintly, aware that Ash was staring keenly at me. "We got him."

Chris chuckled and Ash repeated, still wheezing a little, "Yeah, we got him."

***

Ash watched Stacy give her report to the policeman. He had already given his statement and now sat quietly out the way. Steve and Chris were busy getting the Were into the cage on the back of their ute. To Stacy's surprise, they had first tagged the Were with a microchip between his shoulder blades.

"Can't have him running loose for long. This will help us find him if he does," Ash had explained.

Stacy, using her hands to talk expressively to the police, looked beautiful despite her tiredness.

He knew she minded like anything having her special camera smashed. It must have cost her a fortune, and while she didn't look like she was hurting for money, he doubted she could just go out and buy a new one.

Ash felt guilty. He also felt a new respect for Chris. He had half-guessed when he had seen the big man. It was quick thinking to have destroyed the camera like that. It wouldn't do for something like this to get out. Still, he couldn't help but feel quite bad for Stacy. This would have been her biggest breakthrough.

And he still had to get her photos from the night before...Or not.

He watched, expressionless, as Steve removed a small USB drive from Stacy's computer, spotted Ash's interest, and winked at him. Ash nodded once. Well, well. Would wonders never cease?

Minutes later, everyone seemed to leave at once, and then it was just Ash and Stacy.

With hesitation, he asked, "Would you like me to stay?"

"Er, no. Thanks," she said, distracted. "I think I just need a rest. It's been a hectic few hours."

"Yeah, well. You're right. You should get some rest. If you need me, I'm just a phone call away."

"Yeah. Thanks."

"Well, I guess I'd better follow Chris and Steve to the police station."

She looked questioningly at him.

"I'm still the local forester," he reminded her.

"Oh, yeah. Sorry. Forgot." She smiled. Then, "What will happen to him, the Were?"

Ash shrugged. "That's gonna be interesting. There'll be some debate about who gets to keep him, and how he should pay for his crimes."

"Surely he can't go to regular prison?"

Ash's eyes flickered. "No, of course not. It will all have to be decided, and I'd best be there to represent the interests of this forest. So, er, see you soon?"

She smiled again. "I'd like that."

"Good." Ash smiled back, sketched a waved and began walking back to his ute far down the track.

Stacy stood on the deck watching him lope away. He turned back once more to wave. She waved back.

***

It was a relief to be on my own. I booted up my laptop, anxious to look at all the pics from the previous night again, as well as the ones from that morning and the afternoon. A strong suspicion had just gotten stronger. Chris had deliberately broken my camera, I was sure. He was anything but clumsy. But why?

I fingered the broken camera gingerly. It was sturdy enough not to have gone to pieces, but it would never take another photo again. My laptop informed me the OS could not be found and flashed the C-prompt. Dammit! That was all I needed. I rebooted it with little hope. My laptop had stood on the table. Anybody could have tampered with it.

Fortunately, I had backed up the photos from the two invasions onto a flash drive. And the SD card of the VL-Cam; those things were hardier than most people realised. I placed the VL-Cam's SD card into the other camera from the bookshelf and turned it on.

There it was in full violet light—the moment both Ash and Chris had captured the Were, and I had unconsciously triggered the camera.

All three men in the photo were Weres! The

Werewolf was snarling, his teeth bright and menacing. Half of Chris's upper body revealed he was some kind of wombat thing. And there was Ash's long leg bent and ending in the rather terrifying toes of a kangaroo.

What the hell!

***

Ash knew, even as he turned off the ute's engine in front of Stacy's cottage, that it wouldn't end well. It never did. He had heard it in her voice over the phone. She knew.

And now she had judged him.

A kookaburra gave him a jerky-headed once-over as he walked to the screen door. "Stacy?"

The smell of stale coffee was strong. She was sitting at the dining room table looking like she hadn't slept at all. Five cameras and their paraphernalia littered the table, along with empty mugs and chocolate wrappers.

"Stacy?" Ash repeated, stepping softly into the cabin and closing the screen. It was comfortably cool inside. He unstuck his shirt from his sweaty back and sat down.

She stared at him coolly. "How," she finally asked, "is this even possible?"

He hadn't expected her to be so direct. He blinked in surprise, then countered with, "Don't you want to know what the Werewolf wanted from this cabin?"

Her expression didn't change. "Fine. Tell me."

Ash knew he was just buying time. He wanted to tell her everything, but that would most likely get them both into a whole heap of trouble. Stalling was therefore the smart thing to do. "They told us down at the station that he'd come back for some stolen artefact he'd hidden here."

"Stolen artefact?"

"Yeah. Seems he'd brought it from the States when he came over. It was some kind of ceremonial teapot or something. Worth a few million dollars, US."

Stacy looked like she didn't believe him. "So he stashed some stolen goods here, without anyone else knowing?"

"Something like that."

"And then came back to steal it?"

"He had a buyer for it. He needed it back in a hurry."

Stacy nodded, her eyes still fixed on his face. He knew she wasn't really focussed on the Werewolf and his crimes. She was focussed on him; more to the point—on him being a shape-shifter. He tried not to fidget with a dirty mug.

"Did you know Chris is some kind of wombat?"

Her conversational tone did nothing to soothe Ash's nerves. His eyes dropped to the mug. To lie or not to lie; there was no winning. "Is he?"

"Yeah. And he's almost as photogenic as you under violet light."

"Oh."

Stacy sighed. She stood up then. "Want some coffee?"

Ash looked at her sharply, afraid she was playing some game he didn't quite understand. She looked tired, disappointed, and not a little confused. His heart squeezed out a, "Please," before he could stop himself.

Stacy nodded, swiping two mugs off the table. She took them to the sink. "You're not going to tell me much, are you?"

Ash took a deep breath. "There's not much to tell. We are what we are."

"But how do you become a were-kangaroo?" Stacy was vigorously washing the mugs.

"I'm not a were-kangaroo. I'm a shape-shifter."

"What's the difference?" Stacy stood regarding him, the gleam of scientific enquiry in her eyes.

Ash felt his heart nosedive. He was now nothing but a specimen to be studied and catalogued by the woman he loved. He cleared his throat and met her eyes. "I'm a man who can change into a...semblance of my totem. A Were is less human, I guess."

Stacy frowned, processing this. Then she tilted her head, as if listening to something he couldn't hear before she broke out into a huge smile.

"I guess you are."

"I am." His smile was tentative. "And what difference would it make without the violet light anyway?"

"None." She kept grinning. "But be warned, I'm not quite what I seem either."

"You're not?"

She nodded.

"So what are you?"

"Why don't you stick around and find out?"

Ash couldn't resist the invitation. "I will," he said, getting up and going to her.

He took her into his arms, smiling. He had finally caught his Lesser-Spotted-Single-Female-

Holidaymaker and he meant to keep her safe and free, as he did his forest.

ABOUT LEENNA

Leenna writes cross-genre suspense, romance, and dabbles in sci-fi/fantasy. She also serves as editor to the Myths, Legends and Fairy Tales department of *Cosmic Roots and Eldritch Shores*. When not writing, she often tries her hand at anything vaguely artistic and reads the tarot.

Leenna's most unnerving experiences include: looking a red kangaroo in the eye, flipping pancakes for the first time ever in front of her class, interviewing Alan Dean Foster (even though it was via email), and teaching a hell-hound how to share a biscuit. Sometimes she writes about these and other less nerve-wracking things; sometimes she doesn't.

Find Leenna on her blog, website or Patreon:
Blog: https://leennanaidoo.wordpress.com
Website: https://leennascreativebox.com.
Patreon: Writerstarot With Leenna
Podcast: Way I See It With Leenna

MORE BOOKS BY LEENNA

What's in the juice?

Angie accompanies her engineer husband to Mars to spend more quality time together. But with Kieron working hard, she's got more than enough time to wonder at the strange changes and caginess of the locals. Does the unverified report of an ET visit have anything to do with it? Angie becomes certain there's something in the juice the locals won't share, but what could it possibly be?

Witness to a murder; denied police protection, Sammi has no option but to run. Though the longer she runs, the shorter the distance she seems to be from her pursuers…

Tom and Liu thought they'd made the discovery of a lifetime when the ancient relic they're studying reveals amazing properties. Now, Liu's dead and Tom's on the run with few he can trust. Running into naive school teacher, Melissa, again could be Tom's salvation, or his ruin if he can't stop falling in love with her.

From the deserts of Shaanxi Province, China to the coast of South Africa, Tom and Melissa have to navigate history, dodge the unscrupulous and psychotic, and stay alive to rewrite their own stories. But with double-crosses and fiendish plans the order of the day, who will end up with naught?

OTHER FICTION

I Find Myself Charmed
Three Million's A Crowd
Unsettled
Settle Down Now
Surviving Oblivion
Ride The Wave, Kiss The God
Dear Santa
Foreigners
Non-Fiction
How Not To Meet The Man Of Your Dreams
Your Tarotscopes 2017
Your Tarotscopes 2018

www.ingramcontent.com/pod-product-compliance
Lightning Source LLC
Chambersburg PA
CBHW032019050726
47590CB00006B/2240